TORTURED
BY HER TOUCH

BY
DIANNE DRAKE

First published in Great Britain 2015
by Mills & Boon, an imprint of Harlequin (UK) Limited,
Eton House, 18-24 Paradise Road, Richmond, Surrey, TW9 1SR

© 2015 Dianne Despain

ISBN: 978-0-263-25938-4

Harlequin (UK) Limited's policy is to use papers that are natural, renewable and recyclable products and made from wood grown in sustainable forests. The logging and manufacturing processes conform to the legal environmental regulations of the country of origin.

Printed and bound in Great Britain
by CPI Antony Rowe, Chippenham, Wiltshire

ARMY DOCS

Two brothers, divided by conflict,
meet the women who will change their lives...
for ever!

Army medics Marc and Nick Rousseau
were at the top of their field when they were
caught in an IED explosion in Afghanistan
that left Marc paralysed and Nick unscathed.
Now out of the army, the estranged brothers
are on opposite sides of the country and
struggling to put the past behind them...
until they each meet a woman who
challenges them in unimaginable ways.

Now, as these generous and caring women
open the brothers' eyes to new worlds
of possibility, can Marc and Nick finally
forgive the past and reclaim the bond
they once shared?

Don't miss the *Army Docs* duet
by Mills & Boon® Medical Romance™ authors
Dianne Drake and Amy Ruttan

Read Marc and Anne's story in
Tortured by Her Touch

Read Nick and Jennifer's story in
It Happened in Vegas

Available from March 2015!

Dear Reader,

Back in the day, when I was actively pursuing a nursing career, I worked at the Veterans' Hospital. The patients I was fortunate enough to serve were a wholly amazing and heroic group of men and women. It always amazed me to watch them fight their battles with such courage.

When I was asked to write this book I knew immediately where my setting had to be. It was an honour to pay tribute to the brave soldiers who had once been under my care. Especially in the persona of Marc Rousseau, a doctor who comes home from the war badly damaged. My story is inspired by that of two people I know—people who fell in love despite great obstacles. David is a paraplegic who married his nurse—an inspiring story because the disability was never part of their relationship. True love sees no boundaries.

My heroine, Anne, never sees the disability in the man she loves. All she wants to do is encourage him—the way all people in love want to encourage each other. It's a story of two people coming to terms with *love*, not disability.

I'd like to thank Mills and Boon for giving me the opportunity to show that love can shine through adversity.

Wishing you health and happiness…

Dianne

PS Please feel free to email me at DianneDrake@earthlink.net or connect to my Facebook page or Twitter account through links posted to my website at www.Dianne-Drake.com

Now that her children have left home, **Dianne Drake** is finally finding the time to do some of the things she adores—gardening, cooking, reading, shopping for antiques. Her absolute passion in life, however, is adopting abandoned and abused animals. Right now Dianne and her husband Joel have a little menagerie of three dogs and two cats, but that's always subject to change. A former symphony orchestra member, Dianne now attends the symphony as a spectator several times a month and, when time permits, takes in an occasional football, basketball or hockey game.

Books by Dianne Drake

A Home for the Hot-Shot Doc
A Doctor's Confession
A Child to Heal Their Hearts
PS You're a Daddy
Revealing the Real Dr Robinson
The Doctor's Lost-and-Found Heart
No. 1 Dad in Texas
The Runaway Nurse
Firefighter with a Frozen Heart

**Visit the author profile page
at millsandboon.co.uk for more titles**

To the soldiers
at the W.10th St. Veterans Administration Hospital
and the men and women who care for them.

Praise for Dianne Drake:

'A very emotional, heart-tugging story. A beautifully written book. This story brought tears to my eyes in several parts.'

—*GoodReads* on *PS You're a Daddy!*

CHAPTER ONE

"AT FIRST THERE was nothing. I was running across the field, going after my brother Nick, who'd been given direct orders not to be out there, but had recklessly gone to rescue someone, and the next thing..."

Dr. Marc Rousseau swallowed hard and closed his eyes, as if trying to remember the day that had forever changed his life. Or destroyed it, depending upon which point of view you preferred. "He'd gone to rescue a buddy, and in the end he rescued me. Nick, the irresponsible one, could have gotten us both killed. He shouldn't have done it."

It was always there, always on his mind, if not on the edges, then running straight into it. That fateful day, as some might call it. He called it that day from hell. "It didn't trip immediately, so I wasn't directly on it. Thank God for that. But in the blink of an eye I was cold and hot at the same time. With these weird sensations. I mean, I knew right away there was pain, but I was so distanced from my body at that exact second I wasn't even relating that the injury had happened to me. And in my mind all I could do was think, *I need to help someone. I'm a doctor. I've got to go help someone.*

"It probably took me a good two minutes of lying out

there on the battlefield before I realized I was the one who needed help. That I was the one who'd sustained the injury. The one who was screaming."

He picked up the glass of iced water sitting on the desk of the chief of staff and took a drink. "The hell of it was, even after I knew I'd been hit, I still had to be told. My body may have known it, but my mind wouldn't accept that my body gave in so easily. All I wanted to do was get back out there in the field and do what I was supposed to do, but I couldn't move, except for wiggling around in the dirt. And the blood…there was so much of it, but it couldn't have been mine. There was nothing inside me that allowed for the possibility that I was wounded. After all, I was the medic, a healer who'd volunteered to be there, not a soldier in the real sense of the word.

"Sure, I'd had my combat training, but my job was to put bodies back together, not to become one of those bodies. But I was, and I think I realized it for the first time—really realized it—when they brought the stretcher out for me. The people who worked for me were there to carry me off the battlefield."

"And how did that make you feel?" Dr. Jason Lewis asked. Jason was a kind man, about Marc's age—thirty-six—with thinning blond hair and wire-rimmed glasses. Whereas Marc was bulky and dark. Dark hair, dark eyes, dark expression that belied nothing but torture.

"How did I feel? I felt angry as hell at first. Like, how dare they do that to me! Don't they know that I fix everybody, including the people we're fighting?"

"But IEDs are impersonal. They're just meant to destroy whatever gets in their way."

"Tell me about it," Marc muttered.

"I don't suppose I really have to," the doctor replied. "So what happened after they came to rescue you?"

"They gave me a phone, told me to call anybody I liked. Girlfriend, parent, my brother, who was out there on that battlefield somewhere, trying to save lives."

"What for?"

"That's a protocol when they think you're going to die. I had a back full of shrapnel, nails, God only knows what else sticking in my spine. It's a bad sign, with so much bleeding, and I was bleeding out. My body was trying to die. There was so much trauma to my spine they didn't see how I'd survive it."

"But you obviously didn't die."

"Too much self-righteous indignation, I suppose. You go through these stages like after a death—denial, anger, all that crap. And I went straight to anger..."

"And stayed there?"

"A lot of the time, yes." He shrugged. "Don't like it, don't want to be there, but it happens, and that's something you need to know if you hire me."

"Do you really think that's the right attitude for someone who's applying to head one of the veteran outreach rehab programs?"

"Do you really think it's not?" he challenged the doctor. "Anger turned inward can be harmful, I suppose. But when you turn it outward on your situation, you can make it work for you. The angrier I got, the harder I worked. The harder I worked, the better I healed."

"Did it *really* work for you, Dr. Rousseau? I know you were a top-notch surgeon, and those days are now behind you. You'll never operate again, no matter how angry you get. How does that make you feel?"

"Mad as hell that someone had so much control over

me as to change my life the way they did. I had a plan that got wasted, a life that got altered, and none of it was of my doing, so I'm angry, but I have that right. And like I said, I fight it like I fight all my other battles. It's just one of the many, I suppose. And I won't even deny that I'd rather be a surgeon, but that's not going to happen."

"See, the thing is, I'm concerned that your bitterness will be a detriment to our patients—the ones who want to make it back all the way or the ones who are fighting to get back as much as they can. I don't want your anger or your personal preference in being a surgeon as opposed to a rehab doc influencing them. I don't even want them seeing it."

"It won't and they won't."

"How can I be sure of that?"

"I don't suppose you can when all you have is my word. But you do have my word. The thing is, I've made it back as far as I can go. Granted, I'm a para-plegic now, but who better to work with the men and women like me than me? I mean, I understand what it's like to have your life taken away from you and in its place you're given something that's going to fight you every day of your life. I know how hard you have to work just to keep your head above water. And that's where I'm coming from."

"But will your internal struggles prevent you from recognizing someone who's in such great depths of de-spair he or she might be contemplating suicide? Because we run into those patients every now and then."

"I contemplated it myself for a while, so I know the symptoms."

"What's 'a while'? Define that in terms of duration, if you will."

"Weeks, maybe. I wouldn't work at improving, and all I wanted to do was die. I mean, what was the point? I couldn't have what I wanted—my girlfriend had walked out on me because I was suddenly not what she wanted, my friends shunned me for fear they'd say or do the wrong thing. My family couldn't be around me without crying. My brother was so consumed with survivor's guilt he couldn't stand to look at me—he was an army doc who escaped the field in one piece and he was also the one who convinced me to join up. He blames himself for my condition because he disobeyed orders and ran out onto the battlefield. Finds it very difficult being around me now, even though I understand that's just the way my brother is. He blames himself for my condition because of it."

"Because of your disability or your attitude?"

"I'm not deluding myself, Doctor. It was my attitude, but my attitude was precipitated by my disability. So I turned my back on the people who still cared—so much so they couldn't stand to be around me any longer. They tried and I pushed them away."

Marc shifted positions in his wheelchair, raised himself up with massive arms, then lowered himself again. "There were questions about how much ability I'd regain, whether or not I'd be able to take care of myself, find a new life, function as a man... It's overwhelming, and it scared me, and the more frightened I was, the more I just wanted it all to end. But I'm not a quitter and that quitting attitude just made me angry, which pushed me harder to prove I was OK. It's been a vicious circle, as you can see. Was then, still is. But I get through it."

"Then you're not over it?"

"I can cope with it now. But I do need to stay busy

and find something other than myself to focus on, which is why I retrained, served a second residency at Boston Mercy Hospital, and why I'm sitting here, applying for this job."

"Meaning you're going to take all that pent-up frustration and turn yourself into a first-class rehab doctor."

"Amazing what a healthy dose of anger can do, isn't it? You know what they say…" Marc's eyes went distant for a second, but for only a second. "What doesn't kill you makes you stronger. Well, it hasn't killed me so far."

"I saw your records, talked to your chief resident at Boston Mercy General. You did a good job there, but what makes you think you can translate that into doing a good job here, where you're a full staff member with staff responsibilities as well as administrative duties?"

"I know how to lead, and people do listen to me. And as they say, I've got street cred now. If you came into your clinic, who would you rather listen to—someone like you who's never experienced anything more than a shaving cut, or me?"

"You've got a good point, Dr. Rousseau."

The man was trying to get his goat. He knew that. But he also knew Jason Lewis had the right to prod as hard as he wanted since what he was going to get was basically a brand-new doctor in the field. "Good enough to offer me the position?" They'd been talking back and forth for weeks—by phone, on the internet, texting. This whole interview process was dragging him down. He knew he was a liability—a great big one. But he also knew he was a good doctor. So which one outweighed the other?

Lewis laughed. "I will say you've got guts to go along with your attitude."

"And that's all I'll need to get through to some of these guys and gals. So offer me a job on the spot, and I'll see what I can do to curb my attitude."

"On the spot? You want me to offer you a job on the spot without going to the board first, or talking to the people who will be working closest with you?"

Marc arched his eyebrows. "You've got the power, haven't you? And it's not like this interview process hasn't been going on in some form for quite a while."

"Oh, I've got the power, but I'm still not sure you're the right candidate."

"Let's see. I've got administrative experience, I'm a good doctor, I have practical experience... What more do you need?"

Dr. Lewis shook his head. "On paper you're the perfect candidate."

"But?"

"But I don't want this clinic turning out a whole battalion of *you*. And I'm afraid that's what you're going to do."

"In other words, you don't believe I have the ability to separate my personal from my professional life. So tell me, are you able to do that? Do you never take your work home with you or bring your personal life to work?"

"Most days I'm good," Lewis said.

"And most days, I will be, too. All I've got is my word. I know I've got some attitude adjustments to make still, but that could also be a strength in helping my patients, in making them understand how they're not the only ones. So, on the spot?" He held out a confident hand to shake with Dr. Lewis.

Lewis took in a deep breath, let it out slowly, and

extended his hand to Marc. "On the spot, but it's a probationary spot. Three months to start with, then a re-evaluation."

"That's all I can ask for," Marc said. "Thank you."

"I'm warning you, Rousseau, when you're on my time you're a rehab doctor, nothing more, nothing less. Do you understand me?"

Marc nodded. "So I'm assuming my office is more accessible than yours because this one is too small for good maneuverability?" Inwardly, he was pleased by the offer. Now all he had to do was see if it was a match made in heaven or hell.

Anne Sebastian looked out her window at the gardens stretching as far as she could see. But it wasn't the garden she was seeing. In fact, she was seeing red! "Seriously, you hired him to head physical rehab?"

Jason Lewis shrugged. "He has the qualifications we need."

"And an attitude that precedes him. I have a friend at Mercy who said—"

"He'll adjust," Jason interrupted. "In spite of what you've heard, he'll fall into our routine nicely."

"And if he doesn't?" she asked, too perplexed to turn around to confront her brother-in-law.

"Then I'll fire him, the way I would any other staff member who becomes a detriment to the facility or its patients."

She spun around. "No, you won't. It's not in you to do something like that. Especially since he's a wounded soldier."

"Then we'll just have to keep our fingers crossed he works out, won't we?"

Anne heaved a dubious sigh. "Hannah married a real softie. You know that, don't you?"

Jason blushed. "You do know that no one else on my staff talks to me the way you do?"

"Family prerogative. Besides, she's confined to bed until she delivers, so, as your wife's twin sister, older by eight minutes, might I remind you, it's up to me to make sure things are running the way they should."

Anne was an internist who'd earned an additional PhD in psychology, and turned her medical practice into one that specialized in post-traumatic stress disorder. Her sister, an ear specialist, worked with combat vets who'd suffered hearing loss due to trauma. And Jason was also a radiologist who oversaw all the X-rays generated in his clinic.

Jason overexaggerated a wince. "A daughter. Between you two and her, I'll never be able to win an argument."

"Poor Jason," Anne teased.

"Poor Jason is right. Speaking of which, our new hire, Marc Rousseau…"

"Do we have to talk about the man?"

"Not if you don't want to. But since your office is going to be close to his, I was hoping you'd show him some consideration."

"Consideration?" she asked. "If you mean taking him on as a case…"

"Not as a case. As a colleague who, like you, started over. It wasn't easy for you. Remember? Anyway, he comes with glowing references as a doctor and miserable mentions as a human being. He admits his anger. Almost embraces it. But to get his skills, we take the whole package. That's all there is. Promise. No underhanded scheme to try and fix him or anything like that. Just be his friend. Make him aware that he's welcome here."

"Why *did* you hire him, Jason, when you've got so many doubts?"

"Because he can unquestionably do the job. That's my first consideration. And I'm also thinking that he's one of the soldiers who got overlooked in the process. It happens every day, Anne, and you know that better than anybody else. We get the worst ones, the ones who can't function, for whatever reason. With one in every eight soldiers suffering from PTSD and only about thirty percent of those ever getting help, the rest are living in a personal hell.

"They could benefit from what we do here, and I happen to think Marc Rousseau might be great at spotting troubling issues others have missed. He's perceptive." He raised teasing eyebrows. "And who better to put a man in his place if he needs it than you?"

She winced. "All it takes is a bad marriage. Want to hear my opinions on that?"

Jason smiled sympathetically. "Ah, Bill. The vanquished husband. I could go beat him up if that makes you feel any better."

"I'm sounding like the one with the rotten attitude, aren't I?"

"You've been through your share of misery."

"And come through it wiser than I was."

"Look, I know the divorce was tough, but you never let it affect your work when you were going through the various aspects of it. I gave you the benefit of the doubt and hired you pretty much untested in PTSD because

I believed in you, and I'd hope you'd do the same for Marc. Give him the same chance I gave you."

"Tough divorce is an understatement. It was devastating, discovering how many times Bill cheated on me when I was overseas."

"And you're better off being rid of him."

"I am, but still..." She shrugged. "Look, I know Rousseau by the reputation that precedes him, but I wouldn't recognize him if he walked right by me, and I'm still a little on edge."

"Then you don't know?" Jason frowned. "I'd assumed since you knew he was a returning wounded soldier..."

"Know what?"

"Marc Rousseau is a paraplegic. Incomplete, lower injury. Full sensation, but not enough muscle recovery to get his legs back under him."

Anne's eyes widened. "Bad attitude and disabled?"

"Well, for sure, if you can survive working with him, you'll regain some of the self-confidence you lost in the divorce mess. But the man is worth saving because he's a damned good doctor and I want him to work out here, Anne. We need him as much as he needs us. So, besides your self-confidence, I'll give you a trophy or something for enduring him."

"Damn the disability..."

Jason laughed. "It gets you in the soft spot every time, doesn't it?"

"How did it happen?"

"He was a medic, got hit by shrapnel...nails, wire, that kind of stuff...from an IED. Was a pretty bad injury, touch and go for a while. But luckily—if you can call anything about it lucky—his injury could have been worse. He's pretty independent. In fact, the only thing he can't do is walk."

"And that's not going to happen?"

Jason shook his head. "He's in the chair for the count."

"With a lot of anger issues you're attributing to PTSD."

"He worked through the physical end of it like a man possessed, but he neglected…himself. Lost himself in the whole affair. Which is a damn shame because he saved lives, was commended as a battlefield surgeon."

Anne walked over to her desk and sat down. "OK, I'll cut him some slack, but only some. That's the best I can offer you right now."

"He's going to be spotting a lot of your patients and referring them to you. You do realize that, don't you?"

She nodded.

"And I'm not going to soft-pedal this. He'll be a challenge, Anne, but, unlike Bill and all his affairs, it won't be directed at you."

All Bill's affairs. She'd been overseas in one medical capacity or another for three tours, while the husband who'd vowed to be true had been tracked to nine different affairs. Even Bill's attorney hadn't tried too hard to help him during nearly a year of divorce proceedings. "I can take on a challenge as long as it's not personal," Anne replied. "And apart from a husband having all those affairs while his wife was off, serving her country, I don't think anything could be much more challenging than that."

"I really want Marc stable enough to stay with us," Jason said. "We need someone who's been through it so he can get to others who are going through what he did."

"I know. And you're right. So I'll be on my good be-havior with him."

"And you'll help him get acclimated to the way we do things here?"

"Yes," she answered. "But he's got to meet me half-way."

"That takes believing in himself. And what better way to do that than being involved in his job?"

"When does he start?"

"He's started. I couldn't see any reason to put him off. I hired him on the spot and sent him down to his office."

"Then there was no point to this discussion."

Jason smiled. "You're my other volatile physician, so I thought I'd give you fair warning. Let's just call it a family courtesy."

"Speaking of which, tell Hannah I'll be by soon," Anne said as Jason headed to her door, leaving her to study her surroundings. She loved this place, loved the contemporary chrome look. Most of all, she loved the Gallahue Rehabilitation Center for Veterans for the good work it did. It was small, limited in the cases it could take. But the services it offered, thanks largely to Maynard and Lois Gallahue in memory of their fallen son, were amazing and much more extensive than one might expect from a relatively small clinic. And wait-ing lists for admittance were long.

Rumors had it the Gallahue Foundation for return-ing wounded soldiers would be upping its contribution, and she'd heard other notable companies were making funds available. So, as far as Anne was concerned, the sky here was the limit. She hoped so, anyway, because she saw the work being done every day. Witnessed first-hand the miracles.

"Got a minute?" she asked a little while later, poking her head through the semi-open door that read "John Hemmings" in gold letters and would soon read "Marc Rousseau".

"Depends on what you want to do with that min-ute. If you've come to gawk, then, no, I don't have a minute." Marc looked up at her. "If you've come to be sociable, I'm not sociable. And if you've come about a patient, I haven't even figured out how to fill out all my employment forms, so patients are a no-go as well for the next day or so."

His office was sparse—a desk with a chair shoved into the corner, empty shelves, no diplomas. It was as if the man didn't exist. But he did, and she couldn't help but admire his massive, muscular arms, and the way his reading glasses slid to the end of his nose, revealing clear, dark brown eyes. And his hair cut...longish, over the collar, dark brown as well. He was goose-bumps-up-the-arm handsome, but the attitude...wow, was it bad!

"So, have you had enough time to get what you came for?" he asked her.

"What do you mean?"

"Your first glimpse of a doctor in a wheelchair."

Truth was, she hadn't even noticed the wheelchair.

"That's why I didn't stand to greet you. Can't." He shrugged indifferent shoulders. "Don't particularly want to, either."

"You are a piece of work, Dr. Rousseau."

He stared at her over the top of his glasses for a mo-ment. Appraising her. Taking in every last little bit. "So how would you like it if someone came to your office just to look at your blond hair…?" Shoulder length with a slight wave. "Or your green eyes. How would you like that, Miss…?"

"*Dr.* Anne Sebastian."

"How would you like that, *Dr.* Sebastian?"

"Actually, if a man wants to look, it's not a big deal."

"If you were in a wheelchair, it would be."

"Then that's who you are? Who you want to be known as? The doctor in the wheelchair?"

"Your minute's up," he said, pushing his glasses back up his nose and turning his attention to the mountains of employment paperwork on his desk.

"Then give me another minute."

"And the reason for that would be?"

"Lunch?" She heard herself say the words, and couldn't believe they'd come out of her mouth. What in the world had possessed her?

"Seriously? You want to have lunch with me? Or did you draw the short straw and you're the one elected to be nice to the disabled guy?"

"Believe me, if that was the reason, I'd be the first one backing out of it and running away. And I do mean running because I'm not about to give in to your poor-me-in-a-wheelchair attitude and cop some wary attitude when I'm forced to be around you."

Marc actually laughed. "My reputation really has preceded me, hasn't it?"

"Let's just say that one of your former colleagues at Mercy wished me luck and said something to the effect that it was better me than her."

"If I were insulted, I'd try to guess which one, but I really don't give a damn because this is a job and I'm not here to win a popularity contest."

"Trust me, you'd come in last place."

He actually gave her a genuinely nice smile. "Is your motive really just to ask me to lunch?"

Her heart fluttered just a bit all because of a single smile. "Someone has to."

"I can carry my own tray."

"In our doctors' dining room we have table service. Otherwise, by the end of the week, I'm sure someone would have already dumped their tray on your head."

"Lucky for me," he said as he wheeled out from behind his desk. "And just so you'll know, I'm an incomplete, I have full sensation, full function, except for walking."

"And just so you'll know, I don't give a damn about your sensation or your function or any other *man* things you might wish to confide."

"Man hater, are you? Or do you prefer the ladies?"

"Oh, I prefer men. Just not right now and not for the foreseeable future."

"I'm assuming it's a long, sad story," he said as he followed Anne to the hall.

"Longest and saddest. And the rest of it's none of your business."

"You know how hospital staff talks," he said, shutting the door behind him.

"Let 'em talk. Better them than me." Surprisingly, he picked up a brisk pace, one she found quite difficult to keep up with. Was he testing her or trying to prove something? Admittedly, he did have a lot of strength, and the way he wheeled was something to behold, something athletic.

"Keep up," he said, slowing his pace a little. "I don't know where the dining room is, and I'm trusting that you're going to show me sometime this afternoon. But at that slow pace..."

"Just shut up and wheel," she said as a smile crept to her face. Yes, he was going to be a challenge. Maybe her biggest one ever. But he did have a grudge to work out, and a whole lot of anger he was going to have to learn to curb. Without therapy! Now, that was the part that was going to be difficult for her—just as Jason had anticipated—not getting involved in such a way as to help him solve his issues.

"By the way, since you asked me to lunch, you are paying for it, aren't you?"

"Seriously?" she said, fighting back a laugh. If she did get through to this hulk of a man, Jason was going to owe her big time. Big, big time!

CHAPTER TWO

"I UNDERSTAND YOU met him," Jason said to Anne.

"He sat at one end of a table for eight, I sat at the other. Nobody sat between us. And we didn't talk. Not one word. I paid for his lunch and when he was through eating, he left. Thanked me for my hospitality and simply left."

"But other than that, how was he?"

"Rude, arrogant, obnoxious, fixed on his work to the point of not even noticing anybody else there." Her office was adjacent to her treatment room, and both were very relaxed and cozy. An immediate warm feeling drifted down over most of her patients when they came in, and that was done on purpose. Her walls were medium blue, her furniture a lighter blue accented in white, and the music piped in was a soothing Vivaldi or Bach. Atmosphere made a difference in so many of her cases, and she tried hard to achieve that comfort, as comfort equated to trust.

"But workable?"

"That, I don't know. He's as resistant a person as I've ever met. So this one is going to be the flip of a coin."

"But you'll try, since the majority of your referrals will come from him?"

"For a while. But if I see that he's not working out, you'll hear from me, Jason. And probably not just me." Just as that threat rolled off her tongue, she received a text. When she checked it, it said: "See. I don't bite. Lunch tomorrow?"

Anne sighed.

"What?" Jason asked.

"Nothing. Just an invite to lunch tomorrow," she said, forcing a smile. "Lucky me."

Jason headed for the door. "Just be careful, Anne, and you'll be fine."

"Don't worry. I can handle him." *How* was the question, though, especially since Jason seemed to have made her the one-person welcome committee, probably owing to her background in psychiatry. If the shrink couldn't handle him, no one else could, either. What an assumption!

It was going on to seven that evening when Anne finally decided to call it quits. Long days were her norm, especially since she had nothing or no one to go home to. But that was OK because the last time she'd had someone to go home to, he'd been going to other homes. A lot of them. And it made her wonder how she could have been so truly wrong about the man.

Had she expected him to stay faithful while she was overseas? Of course she had. She would have. In fact, she'd been faithful when he'd been the one overseas, fighting, and she'd been stateside, working in a military hospital. It would have never occurred to her to cheat on him, and now she went home to a big, empty house every night, fixed herself a microwave dinner, caught up on some reading, showered and went to bed.

Big night. And nights were the worst, which was why she put in at least a dozen hours a day at the hospital. It was better than going home.

Flipping off the lights, she opened up the door and nearly tripped over Marc, who was merely sitting outside her office door. "What do you want?" she snapped.

"You bought me lunch, so I owe you a meal. Dinner?"

"You don't owe me anything." Her heart skipped a beat as she did like the idea of eating with him but she didn't want to sound too anxious.

"Maybe an apology for being such a jerk today."

"Apology accepted. Now, if you'll excuse me..."

"Married, divorced from a lousy cheater, work longer hours than any other doc at Gallahue. I'm betting your evening consists of a microwave dinner and reading medical journals until you fall asleep."

"I do watch the eleven o'clock news."

"The epitome of a boring life. Which is why I thought dinner with me is better than dinner with the microwave. Besides, I have some questions to ask you."

"If they pertain to the hospital, ask Jason."

"Don't you find him a little boring?" Marc asked.

"As a chief of staff or as my brother-in-law? Because I'm actually quite fine with him in both capacities."

"Ah, a family tie."

"He's married to my twin sister, so that makes him family."

"And you spend all the holidays with them, right?"

"How did you know about my divorce?" she asked.

"People talk."

"But you haven't even started to practice here yet."

"And like I said, people talk."

"They talk to people who give them a warm and fuzzy feeling, and you haven't got a warm or fuzzy feeling in you."

"Then it has to be the other thing."

"What other thing?"

"People don't see you when you're in a wheelchair. For some reason, you're invisible to them, so they talk around you."

"And people are talking about me?"

"About how your divorce became final recently. Apparently, he's been fighting you for everything, but you won. Left the man practically destitute."

"People know too much," she snapped. "It was an ugly divorce. But since he's the one who deserted the marriage and left me holding a whole lot of hard feelings, and debt, what can I say other than I'm glad he got everything that's coming to him?"

"And you're going to get..."

"First, sell my house. Then buy a nice little cottage, maybe take up gardening. I'd like a cat, too."

"A cat?"

She smiled. "Everything that makes life nice."

"No man?"

"Absolutely not! Been there, don't want to go back."

"Good, then I'm not taking out another man's woman to dinner tonight."

"I didn't accept your invitation, and I don't intend to."

"Because we're not compatible?" That was an understatement.

"Because I don't particularly like you."

Rather than being angry, Marc smiled. "Do you realize how many people actually put up with me and my

attitude just because I'm in a wheelchair? They find
that if they deny me or do something other than what I
want, they're doing something deeply wrong or offensive. The man's a wounded war veteran and it's important to appease him."

"Appease you? Let me tell you, your wheelchair's not
off-putting, Marc. But your attitude is. So thanks for
the invitation but I'd rather curl up with a good medical journal than suffer another meal with you." With
that, she strode away, the sound of angry heels click-
ing on the floor tile. Rather than frowning, though, a
slight smile actually turned up the corners of her lips.
This was going to be interesting.

"Well, then, we'll stick to the plan. I'll see you at
lunch tomorrow."

She turned back to give him a stiff glare, but what
came off was more confused than anything, and she
hated wearing her emotions on her sleeve, as they always sent out the wrong impression. "Not if your life
depended on it, Marc Rousseau," she said, trying to re-
main rigid, although her insides were quivering. "Not
if your life depended on it!"

Anne snuggled down on her sofa with a glass of white
grape juice and a medical journal and a soft Schubert
quintet playing in the background. She wasn't really
so physically tired as she was mentally stressed. Nothing had gone well today. Two of her patients had had
emotional breaks—big ones. One had tried to jump
out her window until he remembered her office was
on the first floor, and then he'd simply smashed furniture. After which he'd apologized and offered to pay for
the damages. The other had sat in her office and wept

uncontrollably for over an hour, until she'd finally had him sedated and checked in for a night of observation.

Shutting her eyes, she rotated her ankles for a moment, then sank further back into the sofa pillows, not sure if, when the time came, she'd be able to get up and make it all the way upstairs to the bedroom.

She really did hate this house. Hated everything in it because it stood for a happier time—a time when love had been fresh and exciting and she'd known it would last forever. And it wasn't like Bill hadn't known she'd be serving overseas when he'd asked her to marry him. He'd be good with it, he'd claimed. There was nothing for her to worry about.

Stupid her, she'd believed him. And on her first leave, she'd come back to a marriage she'd believed was as stable as it had ever been in their three years. But on her second trip stateside he'd seemed more remote. He'd claimed he was tired, too much work, just getting over a cold...there'd been a whole string of excuses, but by the end of her leave, things had been normal again, and she'd returned overseas happy to know that the next time she came home it would be for good.

But when that day came, she'd found earrings in a drawer on her side of the bed. And a bra. And panties. It had seemed, as the days had gone by, there had been more and more excuses for Bill to invent. None of them plausible. Then her neighbor, an older lady, had commented on the succession of housekeepers who'd come and gone at odd hours of the day and night. "Sometimes two, three times a week!" Mrs. Gentry had exclaimed.

One check with the cleaning service confirmed her suspicion. The cleaning service cleaned every Friday morning. Once a week. No more, no less. Her accoun-

tant had verified that with the checks that had been
written. He'd also recommended the best lawyer in Port
Duncan, New York.

"Protect your assets, Anne. Bill's been doing a lot
of spending while you were gone, and if you want to
keep anything for yourself, it's time to lawyer up." Said
by James Callahan, the attorney she'd hired that day.

Through it all, though, Anne had been numb. She
had been unable to function. Betrayal. Fragments of
memories left over from Afghanistan. Things she hadn't
been able to forget…or fix. No, it hadn't made sense,
but it had seemed like her world had been closing in
around her. She'd been unable to breathe half the time.
The other half of the time, she hadn't been able to quit
crying. Vicious circle. Every day. Sucking the life out
of her every day. Little pieces of it just falling away,
one at a time.

She'd almost been at the point of complete breakdown when she'd realized she couldn't control what was
happening to her, so she'd sought counseling. Her condition hadn't been diagnosed as PTSD, but the emotional
conflict had given her a deep understanding of those
who did suffer through it—the confusion, the anger, the
pain. After seeing it on the field and coming up to the
edge of it herself, before she'd realized it, she'd been
in a PhD program, coupling what she knew as an MD
with learning about stress disorders. It had seemed a
logical place for her to be. Where she'd wanted to be.

For that part of her life, she'd put her divorce on hold
and concentrated only on herself. Fixing herself first,
retraining herself second. Of course, her intention had
been to restart divorce proceedings once the rest of it
was behind her. One trauma at a time was what she'd

learned. Deal with one at a time. And while Bill had been a problem, he hadn't been a trauma. In fact, getting rid of him would be her easiest fix.

So then, a whole year after she'd decided to take that fix, he'd come after her, claiming that her being gone had caused him PTSD. Of all the low, miserable things to do...

"But he learned," she said as she shut her book and decided she was comfortable right where she was. "When I got through with him, he'd learned to pick his women dumb and dependent. God forbid he should ever get a fighter again or she might do worse to him than I did."

Sighing, she shut her eyes, and while she expected to go to sleep with visions of Bill in her choke hold filling her dreams, the person there tonight was...Marc. And he was smiling.

"Nice smile," she whispered as she dozed off. Yes, it was a very nice smile to go to sleep with.

He'd been in bed two hours now, alternately staring at the ceiling, then watching the green numbers on the digital clock. The harder he tried to sleep, the more he couldn't. Marc's first thought was a nice cup of hot herbal tea—something soothing. Then in his mind he added brandy to it, just a sip, but the problem with that was he wasn't a drinker. Never had been. No booze, no pills. Just a bad attitude to get him through.

So what got Anne through? he wondered. She seemed pretty straightforward. Even functional, considering her divorce.

"Some people are made to be more functional," he told his orange-striped tomcat named Sarge, who was stretched out on the bed, snoozing quite contentedly. Sarge was huge, a Maine Coon weighing in at twenty-five pounds. He'd been cowering on Marc's doorstep one day, all beaten and bloody, and there hadn't been a muscle or sinew in Marc's body that could have shut the door on him because he'd known exactly how the cat had felt—defeated. So he'd taken him in, nursed him back to health, yet hadn't named him, as his intention had been to turn him over to a no-kill rescue shelter for adoption.

Except the damned cat had these soulful big green eyes that Marc had been unable to resist. So he'd eventually called him Sarge, mostly because his huge size reminded him of an overwhelmingly large and tender-hearted sergeant he'd had working for him in Afghanistan, and he and the cat had become best buddies.

"She's something, Sarge," he told the cat as he pulled a can of cat tuna off the shelf. "And so damn obvious it's laughable. The lady's in charge of the PTSD program, and I'm sure I'm supposed to be her secret conquest." He chuckled as he filled the cat bowl and laid it on the floor at the back door to his apartment—a door never used, due to the six steps down. Management had offered to ramp it for him, but he'd told them, no, that one door was plenty. He lived a Spartan life, didn't need people fawning all over him. Especially his family. He wondered where Nick was right now. Maybe living it up somewhere and doing every dumb thing in the book just to prove he could. He shuddered, thinking about his brother's lifestyle. Wild. Carefree. Nothing mattered. Most of all, he wondered if Nick even appreciated the freedom he had to do so many stupid things.

Whatever the case, his parents, Jane and Henry, had

been ready to drop everything to take care of him, but that was too clingy. No phone calls or texts, he'd said. He was fine. No sad faces, no mother's tears, no over-compensation from his dad. A cat was good, though. You fed him, watered him, changed his pan, and he didn't give a hang whether or not all that came from a paraplegic or someone who could walk.

And he never should have asked Anne Sebastian out, not even for a make-good on a very miserable lunch. What had he expected? That she'd actually want to go with him after he'd been so obnoxious? "I deserved it," he told the cat, who was busy gulping down his food. "I'm not exactly dating material and, God knows, I don't have friends." But for one brief moment, he'd actually thought a couple hours with Anne might be nice.

So much for thinking. So much for anything that resembled a normal life. This was it. A tiny apartment, a cat and an SUV that had been fixed for him to drive. Yep, that was his life. Except he did have a job to add to that mix now. Admittedly, he was looking forward to the work, to having the chance to help others like himself. "Time to go do the weights," he said to his cat as he spun his chair around and went to the second bedroom, which had been turned into a workout room. "Wanna come spot me, Sarge?" he called out. The cat's response was to simply stop in the hall outside the workout room and wash his face.

"Some friend you are!"

"He's interesting," Anne said to Hannah, her twin sister, the next evening. Hannah was now confined to bed as much as possible as she was nearing her due date and she'd been diagnosed with gestational diabetes. Anne perched herself on the side of the bed with a carton of ice cream and two spoons, ready to eat their favorite— vanilla fudge. Even at the age of thirty-five, they were still identical in every way that counted, right down to the clothes they picked out and the food they liked and disliked.

"Jason said he's pretty bitter."

"I suppose I would be, too, if that had happened to me. I mean, I deal with returning soldiers every day who come back just like Dr. Rousseau…like him and worse. I was lucky. All I had to come back to was…"

"How is Bill, by the way?"

"Even though the divorce is final, he's still fighting me just as hard as ever." Anne wrung her hands nervously, then continued on in a shaky voice, "For two cents, I'd just hand it all over to him and walk away, but my attorney believes I'm entitled to my share since I was the one off fighting for my country while Bill was spending his time on the golf course and in our bed, so he's not going to let Bill go back and amend the settlement."

She shrugged, then patted her sister's enormous belly. "Glad we never had children to enter into the mix. Don't know how I would have handled having to have interaction with him because of a child. This way, I don't ever have to deal with him again. I just refer him to my lawyer." She let out a ragged sigh. "It's better that way."

"But children are going to be nice."

"For you. And I predict I'm going to make a great aunt. Spoil the baby rotten, then send her home to her mother."

"Instead of dating? You know, going out, having fun. Have a life. It's been a long time coming."

"But I'm not really going to do the dating thing for a while, if ever."

"You may change your mind," Hannah said as she scooped a spoon of ice cream from the container. "When you meet the right man, or realize you've already met him."

"Who? Marc?"

Hannah shrugged.

"Ha! Those pregnancy hormones have gone to your brain and left you with an imagination as big as your belly."

Hannah shrugged again. "Maybe you're right, maybe you're not."

"You're the acquiescent one, Hannah, and I'm—"

"The stubborn one," Hannah supplied. "I know. But relationships don't always make sense. Don't follow a logical pattern."

"Tell me about it. Look what I fell for the first time around." Anne winced. She'd fallen head over heels in days, maybe in minutes. Had married in mere weeks. "Yeah, well, next time, if there is a next time, I won't be looking for perfection as much as compatibility. Too bad Jason is taken, because I think you got the last good man. He doesn't happen to have a secret brother hidden somewhere, does he?"

Hannah laughed. "Men like that don't stay available too long, sis. I'm lucky I got Jason when I did because it was only a matter of time until some other fortunate woman would have plucked him off the market."

Anne couldn't help but wonder if Marc had been married or engaged or near the plucking stage prior to his accident. "Well, right now I have a nemesis who's going to fight me every step of the way and that's the only man I want to contend with for a while. And, trust me, that's enough for anyone."

"He'll come round," Hannah said, taking another bite of ice cream. "Once he gets settled into the routine, you'll persuade him. Or let's say out-stubborn him. Poor man doesn't even know what's headed his direction."

Anne jabbed her spoon into the ice cream. "I think he's equal to it. And I think he's going to be lots of fun," she said with a sarcastic grimace on her face to Hannah. "About as much fun as a sticker bush with large stickers."

CHAPTER THREE

HIS APARTMENT WASN'T much in the way of square foot-age, but it didn't matter because there wasn't much that he needed in this world and that included space. But he did have to admit that his office was everything he could have wanted, and more. It was spacious, accessible. Larger than his apartment, actually.

"You like it?" Anne asked as she followed him in through the door.

"Are you my appointed keeper now?"

"In a way, I suppose you could say that. We're the only two with offices and treatment rooms at this end of the building, and physical rehab has enough space it's practically a wing unto itself, so I'm appointed by proximity."

"Don't need a keeper, don't need the proximity either."

"Not your choice, Marc. This is the way the hospital is laid out and, as it stands, our offices are back to back. If you don't like it, well..." She shrugged her shoulders. "Too bad. Because I don't think they're going to rearrange an entire hospital wing to suit your needs. It is what it is, so get used to it."

"Look, Doctor, I know you're probably only following orders, but I'm perfectly capable of managing this department on my own. Tell your brother-in-law that if he believes I need a keeper, he can have my keys back." He fished his set of keys from his pocket and held them out for her. "Take them. I don't want this job after all."

Rather than taking the keys, she merely stood back and laughed at him. "You really are full of yourself, aren't you?"

He looked like he'd been stung by a bee, the words shocked him that much. "I came here to do a specific job, and I'm good at it."

"When you don't let yourself get in the way. Which probably is too often," she quipped.

"And you know what it's like?"

"To be you? No, I don't. I can't even imagine. But I do know what it's like to be the new person in the door where everybody's watching you and waiting for you to mess up. I was there not that long ago, and it was as if every time I turned around someone was staring at me or whispering. Probably because I'm Jason's sister-in-law who came in here with her own set of problems. The difference between you and me was that I wasn't so thin-skinned on my way in the door. Nor was I so defensive. I just came to do a job and so far that's what I've done."

"You're calling me thin-skinned?"

She shrugged. "Maybe not thin-skinned so much as overly sensitive. You're adjusting to a new life, where everything is different, and it seems like every little thing bothers you."

"So I'm either thin-skinned or overly sensitive?"

"Maybe a little. I mean, I had my divorce going on

when I got here and it was a struggle not to let it follow me in the door. But I succeeded."

Marc spun in his chair to see her. "I don't think you can compare yours to mine."

"No. I got out in one piece."

"Out of what?"

"The war. Afghanistan. Three tours. I was a major in the army, which outranks you as a captain." She smiled. "Just in case you're interested."

"You served?" he asked, totally stunned.

"Three times overseas, would have gone back for four. I ran a field hospital."

"Sorry, I had no idea."

"Because I don't wear it as some sort of badge. I just come to work, recognize PTSD when I see it, and go to work trying to fix it."

"And you think you're seeing it in me."

"The bigger question is, do you think you're seeing it in yourself? See, the thing is, you won't get fixed, or even helped, if you don't want to. That's the deal with PTSD. You have to be willing to accept treatment in order to get past it, or at least know how to deal with it."

"Well, my injuries are all on the outside," he snapped, slapping his leg. "Something counseling isn't going to fix, if that's what you were going to ask. I healed fine, and I live fine. Better than a lot of the men and women coming back. So save your healing touch for them, Major..." he gave her a mock salute "...because I don't need it and I don't need you."

"But some of your patients will, and I'm wondering if you'll be objective enough to know which ones. Because they usually don't ask, Doctor. In fact, part of your responsibility will be to make referrals to me and that, quite frankly, worries me."

"Why? Don't you think I can do my job?"

"Honestly, no, I don't. When Jason brought your name to the board as someone to investigate, I voted against you because everything I'd heard, not to mention everything I'd read, indicated you were still fighting your own demons. But he out-talked me, swayed the voting members over to his side to give you an interview, and I lost. So here you are on a trial basis being exactly the way I predicted you'd be."

"It's nice to know who your enemies are." He arched skeptical eyebrows. "Especially when they make no effort to hide themselves."

"You're not my enemy, Marc, and I'm not yours. But I'm not sure you're capable of being a responsible colleague, either. At least, nothing you've shown me so far gives me the impression that you are."

"Maybe that's because you haven't seen me work as a doctor."

"And maybe that's because you've never worked in physical rehab. According to your résumé this is your first job in that specialty. You're here straight from your residency."

"So tell me, how long had you worked in your specialty when your sister's husband hired you to work here?"

"That's different. He knew me."

"But no experience means no experience. Isn't it all the same?"

"You're trying to twist my words," she said, struggling to stay calm.

"What I said was that you got hired based on who

you'd been and not who you were. In my opinion, if that's good enough for you, it's good enough for me. Unless nepotism carries more weight than skills do."

"I'm not debating your skill as a doctor. You come with a lot of commendations, including a Medal of Honor."

"Then what are you debating?"

"Your past, your attitude. A couple of people in rehab with you said you were the worst case in the bunch. Your therapist agreed, and said you fought everything and everybody. She said when someone crossed you, you simply shut them out, and that went for the whole team assigned to you. Yet the people who worked with you on the battlefield gave you glowing praises. Which tells me that the *before* version of you is the real you and you're keeping it hidden. Or, in other words, you're afraid to let it back out."

"So you *have* done your homework." Laughing derisively, he simply shook his head.

"To be honest, Marc, I've done a ton of homework on you, starting with your trip back to med school to do a physical rehab residency. Couldn't have been easy."

He winced. "It was…fine. I mean, what were my choices? Take a desk job somewhere, teach? I wanted to practice, and this gave me an opportunity. Who better to teach someone like me than me?"

"Maybe someone with more compassion?" Anne snapped.

"You haven't seen my level of compassion, so it's not fair of you to judge me. And, no, this isn't PTSD talking. It's one angry-as-hell former army medic talking—one who lost the use of his legs and had to change his whole life plan. So I'm not like you, Anne, who had emotional

difficulties because I couldn't cope. If a hysterical out-
break was all it took to get me out of the chair, I'd be
happy to become hysterical in a heartbeat."

She drew in a bracing breath. She was used to being
challenged by patients. Happened every day. Their trag-
edies were greater than hers, their suffering more—
something she couldn't possibly understand, so many
of them told her. But she'd been to the very depths of
hell, too, and she knew what that felt like. Maybe not
in the same way others experienced it, because no two
people went through it the same way. But like Marc,
she'd had to fight hard to come back. And who knew?
Maybe one day he'd finally understand that suffering
was suffering, no matter the form in which it came.

"Look, we have a meet-and-greet tomorrow to give
you a chance to meet all your new colleagues. I was
wondering, since you're new in town, if you'd like to
grab a quick dinner afterward."

"You're asking me on a date?"

"Not a date, but I thought that since these meet-and-
greets are usually pretty boring, you might appreciate
the opportunity to get out of there a little early without looking like some pathetic loser who leaves there
alone."

"Aren't you the picture of compassion?" he said, his
voice perfectly even.

"Just trying to be friendly. That is, if *you're* capable
of being friendly."

"I can be as friendly as the next guy when I have
to be."

"I have a degree in psychology as well as medicine,
Doctor. Want me to tell you in how many ways that
sounded antisocial?"

"You are stubborn, aren't you?" He actually laughed out loud. "And you think I don't know?"

"Go ahead, call it what it is...stubborn. I am stubborn, I like it and I own it."

A hint of a smile crinkled his eyes. "Well, you've met your match. My stubbornness is going to put yours to shame."

"And you're proud of it?"

"About as much as you are."

She studied him for a moment and noticed that he'd visibly relaxed in his chair. Was he all bark, no bite? She doubted that. But she also doubted that his bite was worse than his bark. Marc Rousseau was hiding behind his disability, and doing so by lashing out. It was a typical scenario for an atypical man. Somehow, she looked forward to the challenge. No, he wasn't her patient, but when had that ever stopped her? "OK, then. Tomorrow after the meet-and-greet. Would you prefer Greek or Chinese?"

"I would prefer a bowl of cold cereal, alone."

"I didn't hear that as an option, Doctor. So Chinese it is."

"Chinese," he muttered as he rolled away from her. "I hate Chinese."

"Then Greek it is."

"Hate Greek."

"Then there's an all-night diner down the street and I'm sure they serve cold cereal." She smiled. "See you then, if not sooner."

What had she just done? Actually, she didn't have time to think about it on her way to her group session. Every morning was reserved for private patients who were not

yet ready to face others, and every afternoon was much
the same, except she blocked out two hours after lunch
for her group session where anybody was welcome to
sit in and talk.

Talking was cathartic. Too bad she hadn't talked
more. If she had, she might not have found herself in
the depths of despair after she'd learned about Bill.
But that's where she'd ended up. Too much trauma,
too much death, too many patch jobs that just hadn't
been good enough. She'd held up in the field just fine
because she'd had a real purpose there, but when she'd
come home to face all the things a family practitioner
had to face—coughs and sore throats and gallstones—
she'd broken in half. That, plus a failing marriage and
her whole life had started to decompose.

And it wasn't like her patients back home had needed
her any less than her patients in the field. But what she
hadn't felt was…vital. The divorce had robbed her. So
had her medical practice, as she hadn't felt like she'd
made a difference at the end of the day since she'd
come back.

Sure, she could have re-upped, but she'd have been
assigned stateside this time, doing exactly what she'd
been doing when she'd parted ways with the army. So on
those evenings when she'd been alone and she'd thought
about the direction her life was taking, she'd let her depression out, fretted a little, cried a lot. Until her hands
had started to shake and her mind had started to get
muddled. Then there'd been missed work and missed
days, and weeks that had gone by in a blur because
she'd been unable to force herself to get out of bed in
the morning.

Oh, she'd known it had been depression. But she'd

never attributed it to PTSD. That was for other soldiers, the ones on the battlefield who came home battered either physically or emotionally. No, Anne Sebastian just felt tired and irritable, and she hadn't wanted to face her days head-on. With family swooping in, trying to get her to do one thing or another. "Get help," they'd kept telling her. "It's not an embarrassment to admit you need help."

Then one day a dear friend from her army days had come to visit, thanks to Anne's parents. Her friend, Belinda McCall, also an army doc, had admitted she'd had trouble. Hers had been temper, and outbreaks, and crying jags. Her diagnosis—severe depression.

"I'm just going through a bad divorce," Anne had replied. "And I can control my moods whenever I want to."

"Can you?" Belinda had asked. "Are you sure?"

Had she been sure? Of course she'd been sure. She wasn't a weak person. Only a person going through a bad patch.

"Must be a pretty damned bad patch for you to miss work," Belinda had taunted her as she'd handed her a brochure for a program in Oregon for returning soldiers suffering from stress-related disorders and depression.

Long story short, she'd seen herself in the description—sleeping on the job, listless. Then one day she'd curled up on an exam table and just dozed off in the middle of the day. After the fire rescue squad had knocked her door in, she'd made the phone call. Two years later, with counseling for depression behind her, she'd had her PhD in hand and had reemerged into the world ready to treat soldiers with PTSD like she'd seen in the clinic. So many of them so often misdiagnosed or forgotten. And as luck would have it, she'd landed the job at a little veterans' rehab clinic in Chicago. One run by her brother-in-law.

It had been a fresh start. What a perfect place to start over!

But was it a good place for Marc to start over? Her demons had been put to bed before she'd got here, but she had a hunch his biggest demons were still in front of him. He'd faced his disability and dealt with it as much as he could on his own. Or as much as he would allow. And he had great credentials as a doctor. So maybe he intended to spend his time behind his work, the way she'd tried doing.

Whatever the case, they were a tight-knit little medical community and she wanted to see him succeed. But if his bitterness prevailed, it wasn't going to happen. Gallahue Rehab was about the patient, not the doctor. Still, from where she watched, the doctor needed fixing almost as much, maybe in some cases more, than the patients.

"Cold cereal? Really?" she asked as she scooted into the booth across from him. His chair was folded neatly at the side and she wondered just how easily he moved from place to place. He seemed agile, with a lot of upper-body strength. Someone who spent a great deal of time working out. And maybe that was his physical rehab philosophy, to compensate for the areas that were lacking.

"Makes a decent meal."

"So does a hamburger or a salad. Makes me glad you didn't order for me. I'm all for cold cereal as much as the next person, but for my dinner I like something a little more substantial, like spaghetti or maybe the home-made lasagna with garlic bread or a big chef's salad."

"You don't have to justify it to me, just like I don't have to justify it to you. Besides, I'm having toast and coffee, as well."

Anne shook her head and smiled. "Without standing on formalities, such as waiting for me to arrive before you ordered."

"You were late."

"Ten minutes."

"Ten minutes, ten hours. How am I supposed to know if I'm being stood up?"

Anne ended up ordering the chef's salad along with garlic bread. "Why would I stand you up?"

"It's happened before," he replied. "Someone takes pity on me, asks me out and has a change of heart. Or shows up and has a miserable time."

"Are those my only two choices?" she asked.

"In my life, yes."

"But suppose I want to have a nice time with you? I mean, I did show up, and I'm in a pretty good mood. So wouldn't that allow me a third choice?"

"For about five minutes, then you'll discover how I don't talk much, or how I don't relate very well to normal conversation, and you'll be miserable."

"So, were you like this before you were a paraplegic, or did all this come about after your injury?"

"My, aren't you blunt?" he snapped.

Rather than feeling hurt or angry, Anne simply smiled at him. "Sometimes you have to be if you want to know the answer to your question. And with all the people I've questioned, the best I can come up with is, you're a mixed bag. Nice, grumpy. Compassionate, rude. Conscientious, bitter."

"That's right, you're a shrink, aren't you? All out to analyze the problems of the world and cure them."

"I'm an internal medicine doctor with a PhD in psychology. Which has nothing at all to do with my question. Which, by the way, you're trying to put off answering or maybe you're just trying to make me angry. Either way, if I'm going to sit here with you for the next hour or two and try to make pleasant conversation, I think I have a right to know what's stopping me. So, I'll ask you again—were you always this grumpy or is it a result of your war injury? Something you held inside until you decided, *What the hell, why not let it fly?*"

"You're assuming I would want to tell you, if it were any of your business. Which it's not."

"That's not going to dissuade me, Marc. I've got a question for every bite of that cold cereal you're eating. One question per bite."

"No, you won't be dissuaded at first, but eventually you'll get tired of asking the questions and give up." He smiled. "That's human nature. And whether or not you like it, you're subject to it, like the rest of us."

She laughed. "Maybe I am, but you don't know me. By the end of the meal I'll have it figured out."

"Not if I don't talk to you, you won't."

"You don't scare me, Dr. Rousseau. I work with people like you every day and I always win." She shot him a devious smile across the table. *"Always!"*

"Don't overestimate yourself, Dr. Sebastian. You've never worked with someone like me and, as far as I know, I'm not one of your patients anyway, so none of this conversation matters, does it?"

"This hospital really wants your work. So much so they're willing to bet their rehab department that you'll be just as good as you appear on paper. We're a small facility, though, and we can't let an attitude get in the way because funding is tight, meaning one false step and it can be yanked away from us. We do good work there, Marc, because our patients get more individualized care than they do in most facilities, and we're not about to let one grumpy doctor ruin a good thing. Jason's risking a lot by hiring you, and I'm not going to let you bring him down. That's a promise, by the way. A double-edged promise, because you've got Jason to contend with and I've got my brother-in-law's back."

"That's a lot of family loyalty," he said, downing the last of his cereal.

"It's not just family loyalty. I love working at Gallahue Rehab. Love it more than any place I've worked, and I sure as heck don't want you and your sour attitude to do anything to disrupt that."

The look in his eyes softened. "I admire your loyalty. I bet you were a good doc out there on the battlefield."

"I'd like to think I was. It was a tough job, but it's what I wanted to do. It's why I do what I do now, because of everything I saw in the field. And what I saw when I got back—the way people treated soldiers with disabilities, even disabilities like post-traumatic stress disorder that can't often be seen." She shrugged. "Too many casualties out there, and I vowed to continue the work when I got home."

"It's easy to look the other way."

"It is, but that's not me. I suffered my own difficulties and I know what it's like to need to reach out to someone who understands. I got counseling because of

my divorce and that made me realize just how important it is to build a person back up from the inside. So,
how about your brother?"

"He served two hitches, but he's out now. He was
supposed to come back to Chicago but never did. I don't
know where he is now or what he's doing. I guess he's
living a…different kind of life from me. Not settled
down. Maybe never will. Who knows?"

"You sound bitter."

"Not bitter, just disappointed by the way he's turned
his back on the people who love him most."

"We all have our ways of coping."

"We sure as hell do," he said as he spread grape jam
on his toast.

"Well, however it played out, I'm sorry it didn't work
out for you."

"You and me both," he said as the server brought
Anne's salad to the table.

"Want to share?" she asked. "This is too large for a
single meal."

He stared at it for a minute, then smiled. "Did you
order the large size because you were convinced cold
cereal wasn't enough?"

"Maybe," she answered. "Or maybe I always take
some back for lunch."

"Good, because I really do like cold cereal."

"Because it's easy to fix?"

"Because it tastes good."

"So does this salad, Marc."

"Are you going to nag me until I share it with you?"

"Maybe."

He laughed and asked the server to bring him another
plate. "If there's one thing I hate more than someone

talking when I'm trying to eat, it's someone nagging me while I'm eating."

A smile of victory crossed Anne's face as she scraped half the salad onto Marc's plate.

"Don't look so smug, Anne. You might have won the battle, but you sure as hell haven't won the war."

That didn't dissuade her, though. In fact, she handed him a big, buttery slice of garlic bread as soon as he'd finished his toast. *That's what you think*, she thought to herself. *That, Marc Rousseau, is what you think.*

CHAPTER FOUR

MARC SAT OFF, almost in the corner, and simply watched the physical therapists and others work while he made detailed notes of everything going on in the busy room.

The room had a crazy mishmash of disabilities—some curable, some not. And everything seemed to be going rather well, all things considered. But the one thing he didn't like was the mix-up of medical types. It seemed confusing to him, having one disability type working right alongside a different disability. And men and women in various forms of physical therapy together. Apples and oranges, he supposed. But he didn't want fruit salad. That's the thing.

He wanted order in his department, and maybe one way to do that was to divide the one large room into two rooms. He also wanted private therapy rooms because not every patient needed to suffer their woes in public, no matter how supportive everyone else in the room might be.

He remembered his early days, how angry he'd been. He'd thrown literal tantrums, which was something no one needed to witness. A private room would have done him better. Maybe helped him progress faster or at the very least spared his dignity when he'd gone off in one of his fits. Private rooms were a priority. Not negotiable.

Maybe no one here saw harm in the gang philosophy, and the camaraderie seemed high enough, in spite of all the many different cases, and maybe each patient could get to the point where the group thing would be good. But right now it put him in mind of the field hospital where only thin curtains had separated each surgery, leaving essentially one large room where any number of different types of procedures had been taking place at the same time. He'd hated the impersonality of it then and he hated it now.

"Note to self," he jotted, "change the system. Keep the various modalities consistent with one another."

Easier said than done, he supposed. But they may as well get used to him and his causes right from the start. Because once he fixed on an idea...

"So, what do you think of our main PT room?" Jason asked, stepping up behind Marc.

"Do you want me to lie and tell you how nice it is or do you want my honest opinion?"

"That bad?"

"Worse! I don't like the idea of mixing my therapies. I know you've got a lot of patients who need use of this space, but having hand trauma working right next to a quadriplegic doesn't serve any purpose. In fact, I can see how it might be a disincentive for the quad to do his best work."

"So you see the work as competition?" Jason asked.

"Not competition, more motivational. Or as a way to relate to each other. Right now, it doesn't serve its fullest purpose."

"And you want to change the system?"

"Of course I want to change the system. Nothing drastic. Just something to afford more continuity and privacy. And I'm thinking that'll be my first priority."

"Are you up to that big of a task to start off with, or wouldn't you rather get to know the therapists, see the various sessions in progress, get a sense for what we do here that you might consider right?"

"I'm not insulting your results here, Jason. You have a good reputation. But as for my part of it, I want it better and I believe in hitting the ground running. How much board interference am I going to have to put up with to get what I want?"

"Trust me, Marc. The further away from our board of directors I can keep you, the better. They approved your interview based on what they read in your résumé, and, as far as I'm concerned, I'd like to keep you on paper for them. The less they have to deal with you, the better. But if change is what you want, show me what, including a budget, and I'll take it to them and probably get their vote. But I'm not promising you anything other than I'll try."

Marc actually laughed. "Smart decisions, since I don't always rub people the right way."

"And why is that?"

Shrugging, Marc started to roll away from Jason, but Jason caught up to him for his answer. "I'm serious, Marc. As your boss, I'd like to know why you put people off the way you do."

"Because I'm faster at it than they are," he said as he exited the room. "It's a dog-eat-dog world, Jason, and I'm not about to put myself out there as the first one to be gnawed on."

"I'm beginning to think I made a big mistake," Jason

said to Anne, who was passing through the hall a few moments later.

"You mean in hiring him?"

"In hiring him, in not having fired him already."

Anne gave her brother-in-law a pat on the back. "I think he'll work out once he knows his world here is secure."

"The problem is it's not secure until he comes off his trial basis. If any of the board members get to see the real Marc Rousseau, I don't think he'll be around too long. And I may be following him right out the door if that becomes the case."

"He's a good doctor, Jason. If that's what you get from him, nobody should complain."

"If that's all I get." He turned and gave her a hard, appraising stare. "So why are you so squarely in his corner all of a sudden?"

"Maybe a little empathy. I know what it's like to think the world has turned against you, and I especially know what it's like not knowing how to fight back. He's got his intellect and his abilities intact, but the rest of it hasn't caught up with him yet. So give him some time to prove himself to himself, and I think you'll be happy with the outcome."

"You really are a staunch supporter."

"Because I'm a true believer that you can overcome. I mean, look at me." She gave Jason's arm a squeeze. "And I'll be there about six tonight to cook dinner… Spaghetti is what she's requesting."

"Well, she's eating for two, and she does eat a lot. But she's still having false labor off and on, so I can't guarantee how she'll be."

"She'll be fine." Anne laughed. "Can you believe that

in the next couple of weeks you're going to be a family of three?" A C-section was set for the end of next week, owing to the baby's large size.

Jason's face blanched. "Sometimes it's still hard for me to believe we're a family of two. You do know how nervous this is making me, don't you?"

"You're going to be a great father. Just calm down. Enjoy the process, and that includes the pregnancy."

Jason rolled his eyes at her, then scurried down the hall in one direction while Anne went to a group PTSD session in another. Today was her light day—no personal appointments. All group appointments. Too bad she couldn't get Marc to sit in on one, but she doubted he'd ever do that. Doubted he'd ever agree to a private session, either. Well, his loss, she decided as she entered the door to greet seven women, all with a diagnosis. Early on, she'd separated the genders as their traumas were rarely similar, and so far it was working out splendidly. "Hello, ladies. Glad you could all make it this afternoon."

"Any news on the baby?" one of them asked her.

"Not yet, but my sister is getting bigger every day. She's ready to get this thing over with." For the next several minutes they all talked about babies and childbirth. It was Anne's practice never to go straight to therapy as that seemed mighty harsh, so lately talk had turned to Hannah's upcoming blessed event.

For the men's group, she usually started with sports as a means to calm the general attitude as the group progressed in therapy, not so much in grand gestures but in the little things that added up. Like with Marc. If he were her patient as well as her colleague, maybe the little thing would be to ask him to come along to

DIANNE DRAKE   57

dinner tonight. Then refuse to accept his rejection. Talk
about putting herself out there on a ledge.

"I know it's not your usual cold cereal, but I am a pretty
good cook."

"And I'm pretty good company when I keep to
myself."

"Do you ever budge an inch?" she asked him.

"Not unless I'm forced to. And then I force back
even harder."

"It's a spaghetti dinner. That's all. I try to cook for
my sister a couple times a week. She's pregnant and
confined to bed, and while Jason tries hard, his best
dish is a grilled cheese sandwich with canned tomato
soup, and she gets pretty tired of it."

"So why drag me into what's clearly a family matter?"

"I'm not dragging you. Just extending you a cordial
invitation since I don't think you get too many home-
cooked meals."

"Which doesn't bother me, so it's got no reason to
bother you."

"Do you have horrible table manners?"

"Not particularly."

"Food allergies?"

"None of which I'm aware."

"Then there's no reason not to say yes and come to
dinner. It might put you in better stead with your boss."

"Are you implying I'm in bad stead?"

"You know yourself better than anybody else. You
tell me."

"Well, if I am, that's a new record for me. Normally

people start taking offense after three days, and this is only my second."

"It's not funny, Marc."

"But it is what it is."

Anne huffed an impatient sigh. "And it doesn't have to be unless that's the way you want to spend your life."

"I wanted to spend my life being a general surgeon. But we don't necessarily get what we want, do we?"

Anne bit her tongue to keep her from blurting out her next retort. Why was she taking this personally? She had any number of patients in the very same spot as Marc, yet they didn't rile her the way he did. What was it about him that got to her? What was it about him that actually made her feel angry and defensive? Was it because her patients were trying hard at recovery and he seemed to be happy to wallow in his stagnation? Or that she found him attractive and this was only an emotional response?

Maybe it was because some other therapist somewhere had simply given up on him, which made her wonder under what circumstances she might have to give up on one of her patients. So far, she was still optimistic about that; had the idea that all patients with PTSD could be helped with enough time and energy. But Marc was practically throwing it in her face that she was wrong. That she couldn't win them all. And she didn't like that, not one little bit.

"Dinner's at six. Can you get yourself there, or shall I pick you up somewhere?"

"You still on that kick?"

"It's not a kick. It's an invitation." She scribbled an address and stuffed it in his hand. "Be there, or not." Then she left. Left Marc, left the building and left the bad mood behind. Tonight she'd get to spend the evening with her sister and she surely didn't need to drag that attitude along.

It was nearly six thirty when Anne quit peeking out the window for him. Marc wasn't coming and Jason had told her as much an hour before. Still, she'd expected him to do the polite thing—to call with his refusal, even though he'd declined her invitation in the hall that afternoon. OK, so she expected too much. Marc wasn't like anybody else she'd ever known and she was hoping he would be. But that wasn't going to be the case.

"Sorry he disappointed you," Jason said, stepping up to the front window behind Anne, "but Marc Rousseau isn't very sociable."

"Very? That bush out by the front porch is more sociable than he is."

"Don't turn him into one of your causes, Anne. It won't work."

"I don't know what you mean by that," she snapped.

"Sure you do. Hannah told me you always had a cause…whether it was the least popular kid in the neighborhood to the kid who was getting picked on in school. You brought home abandoned puppies and kittens and spent two afternoons a week having tea with a couple of the octogenarian ladies in your neighborhood to keep them company. If that's not having causes…"

"But Marc isn't a cause. I was just trying to make him feel welcome at the rehab center."

"He doesn't want to feel welcome. In fact, I doubt he wants to feel anything. He comes to us with a strong background both as a patient and as a doctor, and the truth of the matter is I hired him as a doctor, not as a patient."

"And I invited him to dinner as a colleague, not as a patient."

"Look, why don't you go upstairs and help Hannah get ready to come down to dinner? I'll set the table."

Anne nodded. It was time to forget about Marc and enjoy the rest of the evening with her family. She headed upstairs and tapped gently on Hannah's bedroom door before going in. "Hey, sis. You know Mom's coming for the first two or three weeks, don't you? And she's dragging Daddy with her. They won't be separated now that he's retired."

Hannah smiled. "First grandchild, so I'm betting they'll stay six weeks."

"Or move in." Anne laughed. "She keeps asking me if there are any prospects in my future."

Hannah scooted to the edge of the bed and let her swollen feet dangle over. "And are there? Jason said you asked someone to dinner tonight, but he was betting he wouldn't show."

"Jason was right. I did, and he didn't. Marc shows antisocial tendencies."

"You've fallen for someone who's antisocial?"

"No!" Anne shook her head adamantly. "Not fallen. I just feel…he's not adjusting well to his new situation, and I thought a night out might do him good."

"What's his new situation?"

"He's a paraplegic. Took a lot of shrapnel to the spine during the war, and it left him in a wheelchair."

"That's right. Jason mentioned the wheelchair. That he's highly functional."

Anne widened her eyes. "What do you mean, *highly functional*?"

"In everyday functions. He can get around. Do his job. Otherwise Jason wouldn't have hired him as head of the physical rehab department. Meaning he doesn't need to be one of your pet projects, Anne."

"That's exactly what Jason said to me. The thing is, he scares me a little bit."

"Physically? As in threatening?"

"No, nothing like that. More like love-hate, and I never know which one's going to pop out."

"You love him!"

"Not like that. More as a friend, I think."

"You think?"

"Well, certainly not *in* love, the way you mean it."

"Oh, like when you jumped right in with Bill?"

"Nothing like that. I'm too wise to get caught up in a mess like that again."

"You're assuming that Marc would be like Bill if you did fall in love with him."

"I'm not assuming anything. It's just that… I don't know what!" Anne bent to slide a pair of slippers on her sister's feet, then helped her out of bed. "I'm trying to be a friend," she insisted.

"How good of a friend remains to be seen. Now, be a friend to me and point me in the direction of the door. I can't see past my belly anymore."

"Are you sure there's only one in there?"

Hanna laughed. "Sometimes it feels like five or six, but I'm confident it's just one little girl." She stretched. "Do you know how nice it is to actually get to leave this room and go downstairs and feel somewhat human again? I'm so tired of being bedridden." She reached for her back. "And stiff and sore."

"You're not in labor, are you?"

"Same twinges I've been having for weeks. No big deal. Doc's going to deliver me either next week or, if we can hold out longer, the week after. He wants to wait as long as he can to make sure her lungs are fully formed and she'll be able to hold her blood sugar steady. Big preemies tend to have blood-sugar crashes."

"But it could be sooner?"

"And it could be my craving for spaghetti, too, that's causing the twinges."

"You're hopeless," Anne said, laughing. "And I guarantee in a few weeks you're going to wish you'd had more time in bed. If your baby is anything like what Mom said we both were…" She grinned. "Better you than me. So, have you picked out a name yet?" Anne slid her arm around Hannah's waist and escorted her to the bedroom door, where she grabbed her back again.

"Well, last time Jason and I talked about it, he was leaning toward Chloe or Zoe. Mother wants Rose Mary or Mary Rose." Hannah gasped slightly. "Jason's mother has her vote in for Abigail or Gabrielle. And me? I think we should let her name herself when she's old enough."

When they got to the stairs, Anne glanced down, only to see Marc sitting at the bottom of the stairs, looking up. "Sorry I'm late," he said, "but I had to go to a couple of places to find non-alcoholic wine to go with dinner."

"Wow, he's certainly handsome," Hannah whispered in Anne's ear. "I can see why you were so grumpy about him not being here."

"It's not like that," Anne whispered back.

"Well, it should be." She smiled generously at Marc, who actually greeted her smile with a pleasant one of his own, all the while avoiding Anne's eyes.

"It's a pleasant evening, so I thought we'd eat out on the back patio," Jason cut in as he came up the stairs to take hold of his wife's arm. Anne followed them down, took the two bottles of sparkling grape juice from Marc without saying a word and continued into the kitchen.

"Personally, I don't think Hannah should eat right now because I'm betting the baby will arrive tonight," Anne whispered to Marc. "She's miscarried twice and had some false labor and she doesn't want to get her hopes up, so she's denying it, but I think it's a good thing she's surrounded by doctors tonight, because I'm betting there's a trip to the hospital in her very near future."

"Too soon," Hannah said, coming through the kitchen door and grabbing her belly. "Doctor says not for at least another week or more."

"And doctors have been known to be wrong, so any wagers?" Anne asked, cringing in sympathy as her sister's next labor pain struck.

"No way. You're not wagering on my baby. It's not coming tonight, I tell you!"

"Maybe just a little bet?" Anne asked, smiling. "Twenty says the next two hours sees some action."

"I'm not going to the hospital in two hours!" Hannah snapped.

Anne knew her sister was scared to death, especially after the loss of her first two, but in her opinion, there was almost no denying the fact that the baby was getting ready to make her grand entrance.

"I'll take twenty on that for tomorrow," Jason added.

"One hour and I'm in." Marc tossed in his wager.

"One week," Hannah said good-naturedly, before she grabbed her belly and gasped again. "Like my doctor says, one week or two."

"Three against one. I think we'd better call an ambulance," Marc suggested.

"No!" Hannah snapped. "You eat your dinner and I'll lie down here and rest while you do. And think happy thoughts for one to two weeks in the future."

The other three doctors eyed each other dubiously.

Marc smiled. "Well, you've got a house full of doctors, so if you should need any one of them, just ask."

They decided to eat inside to stay near Hannah, and as it turned out, Marc won the wager.

"Would someone mind calling an ambulance?" she asked thirty minutes later. "I don't think it's false labor this time."

"Ambulance called," Jason shouted on his way upstairs to grab his wife's overnight bag.

"Sorry, everyone," Hannah managed to say between contractions. "Didn't mean to ruin your dinner, but this time I think it's the real thing. Finally!" She gasped as another labor pain hit. "Could somebody see if they're coming, and how dilated I am?"

Anne helped Hannah lay down on the sofa, while Marc lined up behind her, in case she needed help. "All I know is that this baby isn't going to wait much longer," Anne said as she took a peek to see the baby's positioning. "Looks good," she said, almost under her breath. She glanced at Marc. "And she's coming fast. Hannah's got gestational diabetes, so we need to be doing this in the hospital."

"If it can wait that long," Hannah gasped as Jason raced back to her side.

"Well, if we do wait that long, I win the bet," Anne said, taking hold of the hand that Jason wasn't holding.

"So what do we do?" her sister asked.

"We wait for the ambulance and hope it gets here before the baby does."

"It's a girl," Hannah panted as the next roll of labor pains washed over her. "And she's not waiting. I want to push."

Anne took another look and, sure enough, the baby was crowning. "Jason, get behind her and support her. Help keep her breathing steady. And, Marc, you take over for me while I run upstairs and get some clean bed sheets just in case the medics don't arrive in time."

Marc rolled in closer while Anne ran up the stairs, and by the time she was back down, Marc was in full delivery mode. "Push," he said as the baby's head started to appear. He looked up at Anne, whose hands were pressing into his shoulders. "Care to take over?" he asked her.

"Looks like you're doing a good job, so I'll just assist." In the distance she heard the wail of a siren, but by the time it got there it was going to be too late.

"Now relax," Marc said. Hannah was twisted slightly to accommodate his angle from the wheelchair while Anne helped her get situated.

"I need to push," Hannah screamed, then pushed again. This time the baby's head appeared, and within another minute, Marc was sitting in his chair with a squirming, rather large newborn in his lap. He handed the baby up to Anne, who did the preliminary exam, then the paramedics, who'd now arrived, took the baby,

cleaned it up and laid her on Hannah's belly for a minute, while Marc backed away. From there it was off to
the hospital for mom and baby, followed by Jason, who
was too nervous to drive, Marc, and Anne, who actually did the driving.

"We did it!" Anne cried as they climbed into the
car. "Or shall I say you did it!" She was so excited that
before Marc was all the way inside, she grabbed him
and kissed him on the lips, then hugged him before she
realized what she was doing and pulled away. "We delivered the baby!" she said breathlessly, as much from
the hug and kiss as from the excitement of the moment.
"I can't believe it!"

Marc flinched as if he'd been stung. "It wasn't a big
deal. We've all rotated through maternity, assisted in
birthing. But," he admitted, "it was nice to get to do
that again."

"This was my sister, though. That makes it different." Suddenly, the full reality of her kiss sank in. What
had she been thinking? Anne attributed it to a heat-of-
the-moment kind of thing and quickly changed the subject to the first time she'd assisted in a delivery back in
med school. "It was like a miracle, bringing that new
life into the world."

She babbled on until they reached the hospital because she didn't want to address the obvious elephant
in the room—the kiss. When they had finally arrived,
she changed the subject to her sister. "She had a lot of
trouble conceiving," she told Marc on their way to the
hospital waiting area. "They've been trying for years
and were just about ready to give up on the idea, but
the last round of fertility drugs took. But it's been a
rough pregnancy."

"With a happy ending," he added.

"I'm glad because I don't think she'll go through this again. I'm not even sure she can. But she's been such a good patient because she knew this might be her only chance."

"You two have a strong bond," Marc commented as they took their seats in a room that was half full of others waiting for babies to arrive. In a hushed voice, Marc said, "My brother and I used to be close when we were young."

"Judging from what you said the other day, I'd already guessed that you two aren't close now."

"Not for quite a while. And as for our parents, I do see them occasionally, but it's…awkward. But, hell, I'm there for only a couple days, so I can make do."

"You don't see your parents any other time?"

He shook his head. "It's always a pity party with my mother. And my old man isn't convinced I can't just get up and walk because I look so damn good. 'Come on, boy. Just try.' That's what he's saying while my mother's hovering in the corner, weeping. It's…"

"Tough. After I found out what Bill had done, I had a breakdown. Mostly I just slept and didn't function at all. Consequently, my mother cried all the time, on the verge of her own breakdown over me, and my father told me to just quit. Like I could." She shrugged. "They meant well, but it's not easy watching someone you love suffer. For my family, that went both ways. So what's the story with your brother, if you don't mind my asking?"

"Damn good doctor, damn careless lifestyle. We don't talk anymore."

"You weren't stationed together, were you?"

"Yes. Nick always was the one who was hard to control. Still is." Marc shrugged. "I wish it was different. But it's not, and it won't be fixed until he's ready to fix it."

"Did you blame him?"

"At first, yes. And I told him so. But I got over that as he was just doing what Nick would do. You can't expect the man to be different than who he is."

"But you never had the chance to tell him you'd forgiven him?"

"I don't even know where the hell he is, and if my folks know, they're not saying."

"You've asked them?"

"Not in so many words. But I think they're trying to do what's best for both their boys."

"Is it right, Marc?"

Marc shrugged. "Time will tell, I suppose."

"Well, I'm lucky that Hannah and I get along so well."

"Damned lucky," Marc said. "Pretty damned lucky."

"Did we wear you out?" Anne asked her sister.

"Something like that." Hannah shut her eyes and sighed. "Baby's got to stay in the NICU for a while until they get her blood sugar regulated."

"How long?"

"Maybe a week."

"That'll give you time to rest up and get ready for her," Anne said sympathetically. She knew her sister would be devastated to go home without her baby. It was going to break her heart, which broke Anne's heart. "And it's better to have her here where she can be watched for a little while."

"Marc did a good job," Hannah told Anne as she nodded off to sleep.

Ten minutes later, Anne said the very same thing to him. "You did a good job." He was in the process of pulling off his soiled street clothes, cleaning himself up and pulling on some fresh hospital scrubs.

She couldn't help but admire his body. It was beautiful. Well muscled. Nice definition in all the right places. Except the scars on his back. They were everywhere, going in every direction—some long and wide, others short and jagged. Automatically she empathized with the pain he must have felt. "Do they still hurt?" she asked him, as she ran her finger down the nastiest of all, the one that started along his spine and traveled a good length of it.

"Occasionally. Which is why I keep myself busy, to keep my mind off it."

"Are you sensitive or embarrassed to be seen?" she asked as she ran her finger across a zig-zag pattern on his right shoulder.

"Not really. It's all a part of me now, part of what causes me to do the things I do. So my attitude is, if you don't like it, or if you take offense to my back or legs, don't look." He actually smiled. "And don't go get all teary-eyed over me, because I hate pity worse than just about anything else."

"It's not pity. It's just that…that you had such a pretty back."

"What the hell did you say?" he sputtered.

"That you had such a pretty back."

"Well, that's one for the record books. Nobody's ever said anything like that to me before. Mind you, I've had other compliments. But my back?" He laughed out loud. "I never know what to expect from you, Anne."

She sniffed. "I like backs. I'm sorry. Sue me."

"I'd rather stay on your good side, I think."

"Well, your good side saved my sister's life and got her baby into the world safely. Thank you, Marc."

"For what?" he asked.

"For being there, for doing what you did… It was all pretty amazing."

"It's been a while since I've done anything like that. Actually, I've never done anything *exactly* like that out in the field, delivering a baby without medical equipment, and it *was* good, wasn't it?"

"Thank you," Anne said again, bending slightly to give him a shoulder massage.

"You can thank me like that anytime," he said, sighing as her fingers kneaded the corded muscles of his shoulders and neck.

Suddenly, she hugged him from behind in what was meant to be a casual gesture, yet it shot through her like a bolt of lightning, nearly causing her to lose her balance, her feelings toward Marc turning so strong so quickly.

"You OK?" he asked, reaching out to steady her.

"I, um…I'm just tired. And a little frazzled emotionally. It's been a big night, but I'm good." She could still feel the heat of him lingering on her fingertips and on her lips from earlier. "And about that kiss earlier…"

"Nicest one I've had all day." He smiled. "All year, actually. But let's just agree to agree that we were caught up in the excitement of what had just happened and let it go."

"Agreed," she said, even though it still caused her

knees to wobble when she thought about what she'd done. "I can't even imagine how this would have gone if you hadn't been there."

"You and Jason are both good doctors…"

"Neither of us deliver babies as parts of our practice. I did during my residency, but never in the field, and I'm sure he did, too, when he rotated through maternity, but to do it in those circumstances…"

"Neither had I, not like that, until I went to Afghanistan, and ended up in charge of a medical unit where every medical procedure was fair game. We didn't turn people away, and a few of the women came to me even though I was a man. They bucked the system to get good medical help." He shrugged. "No big deal."

"Very big deal," she said. Pride swelled inside her for the things he'd accomplished.

"Look, the wheels and armrests on your chair are messy. Can I clean them for you?"

"I'm capable," he said, his voice betraying genuine gratitude.

"I know you're capable. But you're also exhausted, and I was just trying to be nice."

"Sorry. Sure, I appreciate the help. I am pretty tired. It's been quite a while since I've done anything that strenuous."

With that, Marc transferred himself to the bench seat in the locker room while Anne took the chair and swabbed it down. When she was finished, she pushed the chair back to him and watched him make the transfer back with such strength and agility it raised goosebumps on her arms. "So, what's to say we go home? It's almost time to go to work and I'd like to grab a shower and a couple of hours' sleep, if I can."

"Since we came in Jason's car, I've already called a cab," he said as he opened the locker-room door for her. "Oh, and in case I didn't mention it before, you did a good job for a shrink."

"I was scared to death. Probably more scared than usual since it was my sister."

"Scared becomes you. It adds a nice flush to your cheeks."

They wandered down to the hospital's circular drive and Anne sat down on a bench, nearly falling asleep as they waited for the cab. In fact, she was so out of it she vaguely remembered her head on Marc's shoulder and his arm around her, supporting her. But the cab pulled up and whatever may or may not have happened ended.

Marc entered the taxi first, then folded his chair and pulled it in behind him, leaving Anne to sit in the front seat next to the cabby, a young Hispanic man who said he was working his way through college by driving a cab. Ten minutes later, Anne was dropped off at her sister's house to pick up her own car, while Marc grabbed his own car and sped on down the road.

Had she been resting on his shoulder, or had that only been a dream? Too tired to think about it, she climbed the stairs in Hannah's house and slid between the sheets in the guest room. Sleep would arrive soon, she was sure. But on the edges of that sleep, she kept seeing Marc. And he kept jolting her awake again.

He was an interesting man, to say the least. *Maybe even more than interesting*, she thought as she finally drifted off, thinking about the kiss.

CHAPTER FIVE

THE DAY STARTED much too early and, admittedly, Marc felt stiff and sore when he climbed out of bed and headed for the shower. What he needed was extra shower time followed by an extra half hour in his make-shift gym, but what he was going to get was five minutes in the shower and no workout whatsoever if he wanted to make it to work on time.

Sure, he had a good excuse, but in his life, excuses didn't matter. He got up every day and went to work just like everybody else did. No exceptions like morning stiffness because people would talk. And he hated talk and innuendo and speculation and rumors almost as much as he hated the changes he'd been forced to make to get along in this world.

Last night, for instance. He'd delivered a baby from his wheelchair! It had left him exhausted and exhilarated because for a little while he'd just been a doctor, pure and simple. It had made him feel…great, like the way he used to after a successful surgery. They'd needed him, relied on him and his wheelchair hadn't stood in the way!

Pulling the shaving mirror out from the wall, Marc took one look at the tired lines on his face and decided to forgo the shave. Who would care that he had a five o'clock shadow? And even if somebody did care, he or she wouldn't mention it. People were like that with him, let him get away with egregious things because what, after all, could you or would you say to a doctor in a wheelchair?

Nothing, he'd discovered early on. Not a damned thing.

He hated those eggshells everybody stepped on where he was concerned. Hated them to hell.

The physical rehab room was quiet when he arrived. There was only one therapist in the far corner, working on the mat bed, trying to teach a new above-knee amputee how to stand. Balancing on one leg couldn't be all that easy, and his heart did go out to the young man for the future he'd have to face. But he'd made that adjustment himself, had put in the hard work and discovered that life would go on.

"Excuse me," he said as the therapist wrestled to stand the man up and keep him upright, "but I think more emphasis placed on upper-body strength will help compensate for what he's lost down below. Upper-body strength can be invaluable, so I'm going to evaluate his treatment schedule and make the necessary arrangements to get him into the weight room more often. Maybe twice a day and as needed."

"Yes, Doctor," the therapist said, showing clear irritation that her therapy was being called into question.

"You a doc in a wheelchair?" the young man named James asked.

"I'm a doc in a wheelchair," Marc answered as their camaraderie started to grow.

"Well, I'll be damned," James said.

"That's what I said, only in stronger terms, when I found out I was going to be a paraplegic."

"War?"

Marc nodded. "Afghanistan. Got caught by flying shrapnel."

"Afghanistan for me, too. Land mine."

"Well, welcome to the club," Marc said, extending his hand to the man.

James accepted the handshake. "Yeah. And ain't that a bitch."

"We'll get you independent here. Won't be easy, and that's a promise, but you also have my word that when you leave here, things will be different. You'll be able to get a normal life back and do most of the things you used to do."

"How about you, Doc? How did that work for you?"

"I was a surgeon, which I can't do now because of my limitations, but I'm still a doctor practicing in a field that I like, a field I chose. I had some compromises to make, as you may well have to do, too. But it all works out. And you'll walk out of here ready to face the compromises when the time comes."

"It's awful hard to see it from my position right now, Doc."

"I know the feeling, and I had someone tell me the same things. I thought they didn't know what the hell they were talking about, but I was wrong."

"And you're independent, even in your condition?"

"Even in my condition." He smiled. "So do what they tell you, soldier, and we'll get you on the right track. That's a promise. And in the meantime, finish out your therapy session and I'll see what I can do about getting you in the weight room. You're going to need more strength until you're independent with your prosthe-sis." He showed off his finely defined biceps. "I work out every day to keep myself in shape, and since you're going to be fighting a lifelong problem, you need to get yourself into a routine that maximizes the rest of your body.

"Makes perfect sense since that's the life you've been given to live from now on. One of the reasons I took this job as head of physical rehab was that I've been there, and I know what the emotions are. I understand that some days you're raring to go while others you don't want to get out of bed. And I know what it's like to wonder what your life's going to be ten or twenty years down the line."

"Do you ever get over that, Doc?" the young man asked.

"To a certain extent, yes, you do. But I'd be lying if I said it will all go away, because it won't. You are dif-ferent, so your life will be different. But it doesn't have to be a bad different."

"What about you?"

"For me the hardest part was overcoming the anger." He chuckled. "Not sure I've done that yet. Some days are better than others."

"Sometimes I get so damned mad I don't know what to do about it. I want to scream, or punch a hole in the wall. They want me to go into PTSD therapy, but I don't think I'm ready. I feel like I need to concentrate on one thing at a time."

"Well, we've got a great doc here who specializes in PTSD, so whenever you think you're ready to see her—"

"Another doc? What the hell does this one know about it?"

"More than you and me, James. A hell of a lot more than both of us put together."

James shrugged. "Maybe later…"

"Maybe later," Marc repeated, thinking of his own aversion to PTSD therapy. He was a good one to talk, refusing it in any form for himself, then having the audacity to prescribe it for his patients. But every case was different, and he handled the emotions just fine. He didn't need to talk to someone about it. Never had. Physician, heal thyself. Yeah, right. Attend to one's own defects rather than criticizing defects in others. Wasn't he just the hypocrite?

Anne stepped out of the doorway before Marc turned to exit the room. She'd heard every word he'd said and for the most part he was spot on. Amazingly, he had a skillful way of getting through to his patient that she hadn't seen before. Marc Rousseau was a good doctor, no matter in what field he was practicing, but he wasn't good when it came to himself. He recognized the merits of psychological counseling in PTSD for others, yet not for himself, and she couldn't explain that. Had no idea what he had bottled up inside him. But it was going to be huge when it exploded. And it would explode someday, somewhere.

"Were you eavesdropping?" he asked, catching up to her in the hall.

"Didn't mean to. I actually came down to make a patient referral. One of my patients sustained a head injury, and as a result his walking is very difficult. He ambulates with a walker and does OK, but I think he could be doing better. I thought maybe you'd work up an evaluation on him to see if there's any hope for getting him more independent."

"How are his emotional capabilities?"

"To be honest, he's volatile. Bad temper you don't see coming at you. Neurologically, he's had some damage, but the neurologist thinks he should be doing more than he is. Personally, I think he's angry at himself for not being able to get on with his life. I believe that if I can get him past some of his physical hurdles, he'll do a lot better emotionally. Oh, and he's married with children, and they're just about to the point of walking away from him because he's so unpredictable. His wife does love him, though, but she fears for her safety."

"How long's he been here?"

"Just a couple of days. His neurologist checked him in and his wife told him this is his last chance. So the man's motivated one minute, but he fights it the next."

"Sure, I'll have a look. Can you have his chart sent up to my office?"

"Already did. Along with one for a burn patient and another who had a crushed pelvis. Oh, and what you said to that young man on the mat table...very nice, Marc. You've got some finesse in you after all."

"Should I take that as a compliment?"

"Take it any way you wish, but personally I think there's more to you than meets the eye." And right now her eye was a little more than pleased by his scruffy look. And those shoulders... Oh, dear Lord, those shoulders.

Nope, she wasn't looking. It took everything she had to keep her life on track and the last thing she needed was to drag another man into it who had his own set of problems to deal with. So looking was allowed, but nothing else. Besides, there was his personality, which half the time wasn't nearly as pleasing as his good looks.

It was nearly ten by the time she was ready to leave, and from the parking lot she could see that Marc's office lights were still on. It was good to know she wasn't the only one who worked so late. Standing there, watching for a minute, she debated whether or not she should ask him out to grab a pizza or just leave well enough alone.

"You don't need this," she said as she fished her keys from her purse. Having a professional relationship was one thing, but carrying it beyond that…no way! She knew better. More than that, she knew how to resist it. But just as she was about to climb into the driver's seat, her cell phone rang.

"I was waiting for your call," he said. "The way you were hesitating and looking at my office window…I was sure you'd call."

"I might have, if I'd had anything to say," she said in a voice way more surly than she'd intended.

"How about we split a pizza?"

"I already ate," she lied, torn between going and not going. Part of her certainly wanted to, but part of her was afraid of what might come of it.

"It's just a pizza, Anne. Nothing more, I promise. Suit yourself, but I'll be out in five if you care to wait."

"How about we meet at Crazy Jack's for a burger? See you there."

Giving in felt right, and Anne clicked off her phone and studied the light in his office for the next few seconds until it went out, then she unlocked the car door. Once inside, she pulled out of her parking spot and was proceeding to the exit when all of a sudden another car pulled out of its spot and slammed directly into hers. There was an awful clash of tires squealing, cars hitting each other, horns honking. And the car that had hit hers actually pushed her car sideways into the bumpers of two other cars parked in the same row.

Anne's seat belt locked down so hard she thought she was going to die right there from a lack of breath. Once her breathing returned to normal she assessed herself, as she would any patient. Pulse—rapid. Arms scraped and bloody from window glass. She knew she hadn't sustained internal damage, though, unless her ribs were broken, which she didn't think they were, in spite of the seat belt, but she was willing to bet she'd have a nice seat-belt bruise.

Finally regaining her wits, she looked outside to see if someone in the other car might need help and, much to her chagrin, she saw the driver had extricated the vehicle and was in the process of trying to drive off.

"Don't you dare," she choked out. But it was too late. Now all she could do was hope that the guard at the exit had heard the crash and could prevent the car from leaving. No such luck, though. She saw the car crash right through the wooden guard gate.

Anne was gathering up the items from her purse that had fallen out when, from the outside, she heard a familiar voice. "What the hell happened here? Anne, are you OK?"

"Someone hit my car and took off." Her nerves finally caught up with her as the lot guard came running up, and she smacked angrily at a tear running down her bloody cheek. "I can't believe he just drove away."

"I got his plate number, Doc, and I've already called it in to the police," the guard responded.

"Thanks, Gus," Anne said, still batting at tears.

Immediately, Marc tried to open the driver's-side door but it was too smashed in to budge. So, with cell phone in one hand and wheeling with the other, he went around to the passenger's side but was unable to get through between the other cars she'd been rammed into, so he went back to the driver's side and asked through the broken window, "Are you hurt, Anne?"

"Not too seriously," she called back out. "Bruising and abrasions mostly."

"Well, I've called emergency and help is on its way."

Within two minutes an ambulance from the next-door hospital arrived, and shortly after that the fire department emergency squad arrived and went to work to get Anne out of the car. That took only a minute or so, and when they lifted her out of the seat, she naturally insisted on walking to the hospital, but they put her in the back of the ambulance anyway.

All the while, Marc was pacing back and forth, around in circles, around the car. He felt helpless to do anything. But as they started to lift Anne into the ambulance, she held out her hand to him.

He took it. "I'm sorry I couldn't do more," he said.

"More? You helped me keep my sanity. It was awfully tight in there and you took my mind off being trapped."

He shrugged, then backed away and watched the ambulance span the two parking lots. Then he followed. Before he entered the ER doors, though, Marc called Jason, who was still at the hospital with Hannah. "She's OK, mostly shaken, but they'll do a full workup to make sure. Look, I'm on my way in there right now. How about I see her, then call you back with the details before you mention any of this to Hannah?"

"I'd appreciate that. She's doing fine—worried about the baby, of course. So I don't want to heap more onto that until we have some specifics."

The instant Marc clicked out of the conversation, he was wheeling through the emergency doors. Once inside, he went straight to the admitting desk.

"I'm looking for Anne Sebastian," he said impatiently.

"Sorry, sir, but the doctor is with her, then the police are waiting to question her, and she's not allowed other visitors."

"I'm not another visitor. I'm Dr. Marc Rousseau, her personal physician." He had no idea if that would work, but it was sure worth a try.

"Her physician?" The admittance clerk eyed his wheelchair suspiciously.

"Here's my ID," he said, tossing his rehab badge across the desk at her.

"Sorry, Doctor. I didn't realize—"

"That's fine," he said, pulling his ID back. "Just tell me where she is."

"Emergency four, down the hall, to your left."

Marc rolled with amazing speed until he came to the fourth room, where he knocked lightly, then pushed his way in.

"Who the hell are you?" the attending physician blurted out.

"A colleague. We work together at the rehab center. I'm Dr. Marc Rousseau, head of physical rehabilitative medicine. And you are?"

"Dr. Forester, third-year resident."

Marc gave him a cordial nod. Then wheeled past him. "How are you?" he asked, taking an assessment of her EKG and also the IV solution dripping into her arm.

"A little groggy. They're going to take me to X-Ray—"

"To do a CT scan to make sure she's not suffering any hidden internal injuries," Dr. Forester cut in, trying to take the authoritative position, which he'd so visibly lost. "Right now, it all seems pretty simple—"

"Easy for you to say," Anne snapped, then immediately apologized. "Sorry, but when a patient is in pain, the last thing they want to hear is how simple it is."

"You're a doctor, too, aren't you?" Forester asked.

"In charge of the post-traumatic stress disorder program," she said, her voice clearly weak.

Forester grimaced. "I just can't win."

Laughing, Marc took Anne's hand. "We've all had those days," he quipped as he studied the IV needle in the back of it. "And just as long as you get her taken care of, we've got no problems."

"Well, he's taken care of one thing, because I'm just about ready to..." With that, Anne nodded off. Which was just as well, as when she awoke she was going to have to deal with the way her face looked, which was a mess. And she'd had other abrasive pain and God only knew what else. But she was lucky to be alive, and that's all that mattered.

"Is she going to a room tonight, or are you going to keep her here?"

"We'll have her in a private room in about an hour. It might take her a couple days of recovery here before we send her home."

Marc nodded. "I'll go check and see what room,

then meet her there." But his big concern was trying to keep her down, as the doctor had said she should be. Short of duct tape and a rope, she'd be up and about as soon as she woke up. Which wouldn't be good. So maybe he'd stay with her as much as he could and enforce doctor's orders.

Marc winced over that solution, then gave in to a smile. Never let it be said that he couldn't come out on top in the toughest of challenges. And Anne was one of the toughest he'd ever come face to face with.

CHAPTER SIX

"I'M SO SORE I don't know if I'm ever going to get out of bed again," Anne complained as she raised herself up in bed. Her head spun first, then the room spun around her.

She wasn't hungry, either, even though a snack tray had been brought to her since she'd missed her dinner. Turkey sandwich, tomato soup, all good in someone else's world tonight but not in her own. But the thought of hot tea was appealing, so she accepted that and pushed the rest of the bedside cart away. "You can have it if you're hungry," she told Marc.

Marc had spent the first part of the night in the room with her, pulling two chairs together and using them like a bed. "I think I'd rather have some nice hot coffee to keep me awake."

"You don't need to stay here and babysit me. I'm fine."

"Actually, I've been doing some dozing." Not true. He'd been watching her. Watching her breathing and everything else she did while she slept.

"I didn't mean to disturb you," she mumbled in her thick haze. "Why don't you go home where you can sleep in your bed?" Her heavy eyelids wanted to droop shut and it was taking everything she had in her to keep them open. "Before I doze off again, I need to call Jason and let him know—"

"I did, and he does. In fact, he was here for a while. Your sister wanted to come down, too, but that's been put on hold until tomorrow morning."

"She's good?"

"She's doing great. They'll probably release her tomorrow some time."

"You did such an amazing job…" Her eyelids finally fluttered shut. But somewhere in her deep haze she managed to remember something. "Need a car rental. Have to arrange that tomorrow."

"But you won't need it tomorrow. Probably not for a few days, with the meds they've got you on. So for now, concentrate on how lucky you are to be alive and relatively uninjured."

"Marc, were you able to feel the shrapnel from the IED?" she asked out of the blue.

"Why?"

"No reason. Mostly just curiosity. Because I felt the glass shards in my arm and they hurt."

"I had excruciating pain in places for a good long while. It was managed with pain meds, but as the pain went away, more damage surfaced." He shrugged. "And this is what I got. But I do feel pain in other areas, just not enough to stop me."

"So was physical rehab hard for you?"

"It was, and was the hardest thing I've ever had to do. And when I give up or slack off, it's difficult to regain what I lose, so I guess you could say I'm a slave to my rehab."

"Is that why you chose physical rehab medicine as a specialty?" Her eyelids started to droop again, though she fought hard against the sleep that wanted to over-take her. But she didn't want to go to sleep, not yet. She was…afraid. Afraid of the dark, and the loss of control she'd have over herself and her surroundings when she slept. So she talked instead of giving in.

"Because I have experience, partly. Because I know how important it is on a regular basis, mostly."

"But do you like it?"

"Let's just say I don't hate it. It wasn't my first choice, but it was a field that was wide open to me and it's growing on me every day."

She sighed heavily. "So do you find it annoying when you hear someone like me complain because I'm in pain? Because I do complain."

"Yes, you do. And, no, I don't get upset. I mean, right now, when I look at your face and the way it's banged up, it makes me cringe to think about how much that must hurt."

"My face is that bad?" Her eyelids popped back open fully and she pulled the bedside tray over to her and flipped it open to the mirror inside. "Wow," she said, running her hands lightly over the cuts and scrapes. "That's pretty bad. I guess the painkiller has been numbing more than my pain."

"But it will heal."

"With scars," she said glumly. "Do you think I'll need plastic surgery?"

"Probably not. Facial lacerations tend to look worse than they are. And yours are more scrapes and bruises than anything else. Nothing that's going to mar your pretty face."

"But what if I do need it? I know it sounds trite after

what you've been through, but the thought of having surgery scares me to death."

He took hold of her hand and gave it a sympathetic squeeze.

"There nothing to it. You go to sleep, and you wake up later on." He smiled. "I've had seven surgeries and done hundreds, so I'm a bit of an expert here, on both sides of it."

"Seven?"

"Some were minor. Five were major. The worst part is the recovery room, where all you want to do is go back to your room and sleep, and they won't let you."

"Maybe I won't need surgery," she said hopefully as Marc straightened up, stretched, and transferred to his wheelchair.

"And maybe if you do, it won't be such a major trauma having someone there with you who's been through it all before."

"Meaning you?"

"Meaning I'm going to go grab a pair of scrubs from supply to sleep in and get myself cleaned up and ready for tomorrow. I'll be back in a few minutes."

True to his word, Marc returned with clean scrubs and went straight to the bathroom, shut the door and left Anne out in the room to wonder just how much function he had. In her mind, Anne saw Marc as having full function except for the use of his legs. Maybe that's the way it was or maybe that's the way she wanted him to be. Whatever the case, she could picture him in the shower, water running over his chest, his hair slicked back. And here she was, in rough shape, thinking about that! Shameful. Absolutely shameful. But as she lay back, the image refused to go away, and the only reason she could see for her condition was that her pain meds were making her not only pain-free but delusional... yes, that had to be it. She was...

By the time Marc emerged from the bathroom, Anne was fast asleep. So before he made himself comfortable in his makeshift bed next to her, he bent over and gave her a light kiss on the forehead. "Sweet dreams," he said, then prepared to sleep there for the night. No reason not to, he told himself.

But as he looked at her, her skin so pale against the white sheets, he knew he was treading on thin ice. Anne was an intriguing, beautiful woman and he loved the challenge of her. She probably wouldn't have been his type before his accident, as those women had been fast in and out his swinging door. But Anne would have been the keeper. Except a man in his condition didn't get to keep. There'd be no fairness in it; not for either one of them.

He brushed the hair back from her face and reconciled himself to a long, sleepless night and lots and lots of thoughts about the woman he couldn't have, even if she'd have him.

"Come on, Anne. Wake up. You've got to eat something or they're going to force-feed you through a tube. A great big one about the size of a garden hose."

She opened her eyes, expecting to find Marc there, wet from his shower, but much to her surprise, all she found was her sister in a chair, sitting next to her bed.

"I'm serious. They're going to stick in a feeding tube if you refuse to eat your dinner."

"Dinner? Where did lunch go? And breakfast?"

"You slept through them. Moaned a couple of times, but never really woke up."

"I was tired."

"You wanted Marc. His was the name you moaned."

"But he didn't hear me, did he?"

"Don't know. He left right after breakfast—had patients to see. Said he'd be back tonight. So unless you want him to see you with a feeding tube up your nose..." Hannah pushed the dinner tray in her sister's direction "...you'd better make an attempt."

It was meat loaf and mashed potatoes. "I'd rather have fruit."

"Quit complaining and eat," Hannah ordered.

"How about you eat it, then we'll say I did?" Anne tried to persuade her twin.

"How about you eat it and I'll report that you were a good girl?"

Anne huffed out an impatient sigh. "I'll eat, but I want to hear everything about the baby, like what did you finally name her?"

"Baby's doing well. Breathing on her own, eating like a little pig. Her blood sugar seems to be leveling and we named her Anne Miranda."

"What? You named her after me?" Anne Miranda Lewis.

"Yes, but we're calling her Annie."

"I don't know what to say except I'm flattered." Truly touched, she reached across and hugged her sister. "Why?"

"Because when we were little girls we always promised we'd name our babies after each other."

"But I never thought..."

"You know you're going to owe me one, don't you?

But in the meantime…eat!" Hannah picked up a spoon and scooped up some mashed potatoes, then handed it to Anne.

"Not so bad," she said. "Not so good, either."

Hannah laughed. "Maybe I can come and cook for you after you get home."

"I want to go home. Tomorrow, if I can. Which is the only reason I'm eating this stuff. But let me warn you, I don't want your cooking." She wrinkled her nose in jest. "If I have anything to say about it, we'll order takeout."

"Even though you're insulting me and all I can do is sit here and take it, you're looking good, Anne. All things considered, you were very lucky." Hannah brushed back a tear sliding down her cheek. "Jason prepared me for the worst but…"

"After I heal, we may not be so identical anymore," Anne said.

"Or we may. Who knows? And who cares if you end up with a scar or two? I sure don't."

"Well, however I turn out, I can't wait to see Annie. As soon as they let me out of bed…"

"Which won't be until tomorrow," Marc said on his way in the door.

"I think I'll take this as my cue to leave. Besides, Annie's feeding time is coming up." Rather than walking out on her own, though, she called Jason, who appeared from out of nowhere to take his wife back to her room. "And I'll see if we can bring her down here this evening for a couple of minutes."

"I'd love that!" Anne cried. "Please, try."

"No promises."

"They're pretty close, aren't they?" Marc asked, surveying the empty food tray after Jason and Hannah had left.

"Soul mates."

"How does someone do that? You know, find a soul mate."

"Don't ask me," Anne quipped. "I tried and muffed it pretty badly. A husband who cheated as much as mine did, let's just say that's a reflection on me, too. Meaning I'm not an expert."

"Your husband was a jackass."

"I'll have to agree with you on that. I was a pretty good wife for the time we had together, and if I'd had any inclination that going overseas would cause such a great divide between us…"

"You'd have gone anyway."

"He did marry an army doctor," she said, "and he knew what he was getting. I was honest with him about that, but what he wasn't honest about was his need for a long line of women outside our door the instant I was gone."

"Did I say jackass? I meant downright stupid."

She laughed. "Another point about which we can agree. But it's done, I got out, I'm a better woman for the experience. At least, that's what I keep telling myself."

"But did it make you stronger?"

She nodded.

"And wiser?"

She nodded again.

"Then I'd say it was a hard lesson to learn but a good one."

"I agree. But at least Hannah and Jason are getting it right. And he really stood by her through her bout with infertility and all the treatments she had to take

in order to get pregnant. He was so...solid for her."
The kind of solidity she wanted in a man next time. If
it ever happened...

"Well, they're lucky to have each other. And it shows.
So now, how about you swing your legs back up and
rest for a while?"

"But I'm not tired."

"Be a good girl, follow doctor's orders and you might
get sprung from this place by tomorrow afternoon."

"Is that a promise?"

"Not a promise. More like a bribe."

"I'm usually more alert, Marc. I was in the army,
went through combat training, came through without
a scratch, then to have this happen here..." She swiped
back an angry tear. "I should have seen it coming at
me."

"Well, the good news is they caught the culprit. A
kid who had no call to be driving. He panicked when
he hit you and the rest, shall we say, is going to get his
driver's license suspended. Plus his parents are going to
make him pay for the insurance claim." He grimaced.
"It's hard to be so young, and showing off for your
girlfriend."

"His girlfriend?"

Marc nodded. "She was in the car, too."

Anne cringed. "Oh, that's rough. But somebody
could have been seriously injured or killed."

"Not as rough as a hit-and-run offense could have
been if they'd treated him like an adult. He's lucky
they're charging him with a juvenile offense because
it could have gone the other way then he'd go to jail."

"Lucky," she said, as Marc reached over and ran a
tender thumb across her scraped jaw.

"Boys with too much testosterone and not enough sense don't learn. Some of the things Nick and I used to do when we were younger would curl your hair." He smiled fondly. "We were always in trouble for one thing or another. Boy stuff mostly. Never anything harmful. Stuff like digging up Mrs. Wagner's garden one night. She'd just got it planted, and she'd actually used a map she'd drawn to lay out the colors and patterns. So Nick and I waited patiently until after she'd gone to bed and we…shall we say…replanted her entire garden so nothing matched the way she'd diagramed it."

"What did she do when she found it?"

"She left it to grow as we planted it, knew it was us, of course, and our parents volunteered us to help around her house, mowing the yard, weeding the garden, running errands. Our payback pretty much used up our entire summer school vacation. And while the look belonged in the jungle it was so mismatched, it really was pretty. Next year she paid Nick and me to plant her garden according to her diagram, I suppose because she assumed if we saw how difficult and time-consuming it was, we'd never mess with her garden again."

"Did you?"

"Hell, no! It took us three days to plant it the right way—she measured out each plant in each row with a ruler, and we weren't about to go back and redo it." He chuckled. "We lived an adventurous life, I guess you could say. Not bad kids but on the verge of it."

"You really miss him, don't you?"

"I do, but he made his choice. Oh, and don't get me wrong. Nick's not a bad guy. We just don't see things the same way."

She reached across and stroked his cheek. "I'm sorry for your loss," she said. "And for Nick's, too."

"Life happens," he said.

"You're very pragmatic."

"About some things. Stuff happens to the best of them," he said, smiling. "Look, I've got to get back to work if you're OK to stay here by yourself."

"I'm not that big a baby. Just a little shaken one, but I'll be fine. Go to work."

"Good, because I've got two more new patients to evaluate today still, and more of that ton of paperwork to catch up on. So give me a call if they change their minds and spring you this afternoon and I'll come and get you."

"I can catch a cab just as easily."

"You afraid of my driving?"

"Not afraid. It's just that—"

"You assumed I didn't, or couldn't, and you're not flexible enough to allow yourself, even for a moment, to think that there are things I can do you never counted on."

"I didn't assume anything of the sort. And it's not always about you, Marc. The thing is, I didn't want to interrupt your day. I've already put you out enough and I didn't want one more incident on my mind."

"Yeah, I'll bet. Who in their right mind would want a paraplegic to drive them. Right?" With that, he spun and wheeled out of the room, leaving Anne to vow that even if he had the last car on earth, she wouldn't let him be the one to drive her home. Not with his attitude. No, she'd catch a taxi instead.

And she did. True to Marc's words, she was released the next day without fuss or muss, and went down to the pediatric ward to say goodbye to Hannah, who'd already been released and was back to visit Annie. Even as tired and sore as Anne was, she called a cab to take her home.

Once there, though, all the energy seemed to drain from her on her way up the sidewalk and she was forced to take a seat on the cement bench outside her door just to dig through her purse to find her key. It was like she couldn't move another inch, like her body had gone as far as it was going to take her. So she gave in to defeat and just sat there looking lost and forlorn.

At least, that's what Marc saw as he rolled up the sidewalk in her direction. And his heart did go out to her, seeing her defeated this way.

"You OK?" he asked gently.

"Just so tired."

"You should be. You've had a rough couple of days."

She swiped at tears of frustration and embarrassment running down her cheeks. "What are you doing here?"

"I heard you'd been released and since you didn't wait for me to take you, I thought I'd better come and see how you're doing. Which isn't so well, is it?"

She sniffled and shook her head. "I thought I could do this by myself but I was wrong."

He took her purse from her hands and fished the keys out for her. "Mind if I help you a little?"

"You don't need to waste your time on me."

"I've asked for help when I've needed to. Look, Anne, while I was recovering I had the gruffest therapist who had no compunction whatsoever about kicking me in the butt when I needed it. Physical therapist, not a clinical therapist for PTSD. Anyway, he wouldn't let up. Wouldn't let me rest. Wouldn't budge an inch from his position. It was the most grueling few months I've ever spent in my life and I'll admit I thought about quitting more than once."

"Why didn't you?"

"Because I needed somebody on my side. And he was, even though I couldn't see it very often." He chuckled. "I threatened to get a tattoo where he left his bootprint. But, seriously, you've just been through a major trauma and you need some help right now." He unlocked the door and helped Anne to her feet. "Sometimes, though, pride just gets in the way."

"Like today."

"It's good that you want to be so independent, but don't let it be to your detriment. Now, go inside, lie down on the sofa and I'll make you a pot of tea. No arguments."

"Not from me when it sounds like just what I need."

Within two minutes, Anne was reclining on her sofa while Marc puttered about in the kitchen, putting the water in the kettle to boil. It was a nice, cozy scene and she was glad he'd come in spite of her stubbornness.

By the time Marc delivered the tea, Anne was fast asleep. So he gathered some paperwork from his SUV and made himself comfortable across from her, in her recliner chair, and spent the rest of the evening keeping a watchful eye on her and enjoying the feeling of looking after her.

She wasn't helpless—not by a long shot. And she would have gained her strength back and gotten into the house without him, but it was nice knowing he had helped, and that he *could* help the most stubborn woman he'd ever met. Yes, it was very nice.

"You OK?" he asked two hours later, when she finally woke up.

She nodded and got out a strangled "Fine."

"Want me to stay for a little while?"

"No, you've done enough. And I think I want to go to bed."

"Are you sure?"

"I'm sure. And…thank you for everything you've done. I appreciate it, Marc. Even though we don't always get along, I really do appreciate it."

He cocked an odd smile. "I thought this *was* getting along."

"It's a reasonable facsimile. You're quite sympathetic when it comes to helping others, but you're brutal when it comes to helping yourself. Why is that? Why can't you treat yourself as well as you do your patients? Or even me. I mean, every soldier leaves something behind of himself on the battlefield and carries something extra home he doesn't need or want. And it's not like I'm telling you something you don't already know."

"So I do what? Take a session or two from you and make things all better? In case you've forgotten, there's nothing you or anyone can do to give me what I left behind or make up for what I brought home. Trust me, I don't need you counseling me in the open, on the sly, or any other way you can figure out."

Anne sighed with impatience. "You think I would do that?" she asked indignantly. "Sneak in some counseling somewhere? Counsel you without your consent? Or even counsel you at all, for that matter? You've got no right to accuse me of—of doing something I wouldn't do."

"But you're a counselor, and you know how often

it happens. Someone decides one little piece of advice is all you need. One little piece gives way to another, then another. One is never enough. If I let you get your hooks in me, you're not going to let go without a fight."

"My *hooks*!" She folded her arms sharply across her chest. "You've got to be kidding. You actually think I want to get my hooks into you?" Why was he angry with her all of a sudden? She hadn't tried counseling him—at least, not to her knowledge. Wouldn't try. Yet he didn't trust her. And the thing that had her wondering most was why he had such an aversion to therapy. Maybe it was her. Maybe she was blurring the boundaries between personal and professional and hadn't even realized it.

She shut her eyes and drew in a ragged breath. So what was she doing? Reliving Bill again? Trying to mold Marc into the image of who she'd want, if she wanted someone?

"Don't you?" he asked, interrupting her thoughts.

"I'd like to see you get some counseling, and I'll admit that. But that's because you've got a bad attitude stemming from low self-esteem."

"*Aha!* There it is. One little hook going in." He faked the gesture of removing a hook from his arm and holding it out for her to see. "I win, Doctor. You lose."

She shook her head, almost sadly. "I won once, Doctor. I had an emotional breakdown and came through it because I sought help—the kind of help you need to find."

"Because of your war experiences?" he asked, suddenly concerned.

"Because of my war experiences topped off by coming home to a life I didn't expect. We'd made this life plan, only he forgot to mention the part where I was pushed away and humiliated. But the thing is, I knew I was breaking down. The cause didn't matter. The condition did. To begin with, I can't even start to describe how much I didn't trust men after that. It was like they were all flawed in some way. So I checked into a clinic when I wanted to be strong again. When I wanted to trust again."

"Did it work for you?"

"Most of the way. I don't look at all men and see Bill. But I may come on a little strong personally just to compensate for what I lost, and if that's what I've been doing to you, I'm sorry."

"Look, I'm sorry about the hooks remark."

"You should be." Her lips curled up into a smile. "At best I have claws—tiny little claws."

"You don't take an apology well, do you?"

"Oh, I accept your apology. But at the risk of being accused of snagging you with another hook, let's just say that in my practice I've encountered worse than you."

"Worse than me? How so?"

"Broken nose once. He was the sweetest, most quiet little man… He'd been a clerk stateside and took tons of ridicule for his position. Anyway, he always sat there and smiled, then one day something triggered him and, wham, black eyes and a broken nose. I considered it progress, that he was finally coming out of his shell."

"I don't like fighting with you, Anne."

"Then prove it. Quit fighting."

"Just like that?" He snapped his fingers.

"Yep. Just like that." She snapped her own fingers. "Now, if you'll excuse me, I'm tired and I'm going to go to bed. Thank you for looking out for me, though. You're a good nurturer, though a real bastard some-times."

He chuckled. "Call me if you need anything. And I mean it!" Then he retreated down the sidewalk to his SUV. Climbed with the skill of an athlete into the front seat and pulled the wheelchair into the passenger seat next to him. It all seemed too easy. In fact, everything he did physically seemed so easy, she could see why Jason had chosen him as head of physical rehab. There was a lot Marc could teach them. A lot he could teach her, as well. And she did so want to be taught. By Marc.

CHAPTER SEVEN

"I'M SURPRISED YOU'VE come back to work this soon," Marc said, catching up to Anne in the main hall of the rehab center. "It's only been a couple of days."

"Two days too long," she quipped. "I hate being side-lined."

"Are you OK?"

"Other than a headache and stiff muscles, I'm fine, and it's better being here, keeping myself occupied, than staying at home alone, dwelling on it." Getting grumpier every time it ran through her head, which was about a hundred times an hour.

"Good thinking. When I was injured I was infinitely better off being somewhere other than at home, by my-self. So when the time came for me to start functioning on my own, I was so…I guess you could say preoccu-pied with things that weren't helping me during my therapy—things like sleeping all the time or going on TV jags and watching for twenty-four hours straight—that I quit functioning altogether and ended up back in the rehab hospital." He shrugged. "There are a hell of a lot of ways to sabotage ourselves, I discovered. And I think I took a journey through each one of them. Until I started to swim and discovered an aptitude for that. It's what made the difference in my life, I think."

"But my injury is just a bump on the head and some abrasions. Your situation was so different."

"Different, or the same, it's all about feeling violated. Or angry because you were wronged."

"On different scales," she commented. As they approached the door to her office, she stopped. "Look, I don't remember whether or not I thanked you for all the help. But thank you, Marc. In your own unique way you were a great comfort to me." She bent and kissed him on the cheek. A kiss that was long overdue.

"I don't like gushy," he said evenly.

"I didn't figure that you did, but I had to thank you."

"So I'm thanked. Now, can we get off it?"

Anne laughed. "You certainly don't take praise very well, do you?"

"I don't need praise for doing what anybody would have done."

Like spending the night next to her in the hospital room? And the kiss? That had been way above and beyond the call of duty. But maybe he thought she didn't remember. Heaven knew, she wasn't about to bring it up as there was no way to know what would set him off.

"Anyway, it's good to be back to work, so..." She stepped through her office door and looked back at him. "In my time off I read a couple of articles on water therapy and I'm wondering if it could also help certain PTSD patients—especially now that I know you have all that great experience swimming."

"PTSD as in me?" he grumbled.

"Not you, per se. But it wouldn't hurt you. The thing

is, I was referring to swim therapy in conjunction with my PTSD patients."

"Meaning me again? Get me in the pool and fix me?"

"That's not what I meant! I was just saying that some of my PTSD patients could benefit from swimming. I just wanted you to supervise them or train them if they're not used to being in a pool." She sighed. "How many times do I have to tell you...it's not about you. Anyway, I usually have lunch about one in the doctors' dining room, if you're interested in joining me. Maybe we can go over some of the benefits of water therapy for people other than you. If not, I'll understand and maybe we can do it another time."

"Have a good day," he said. Nothing else. Then he wheeled off in the direction of the therapy room, and immediately regretted his outburst. Sure, he was a little overly sensitive on the subject, but did that mean he had to take everything she said personally? Truth was, he believed she was trying to be helpful to her patients by offering water therapy, and he'd practically laid himself out there on the sacrificial altar to help her, then taken offense when she'd asked. Damn it, anyway!

Anne sat down at her desk and closed her eyes. Well, so much for trying to be polite. It rolled right off him like water off a duck's back, apparently. But why? What kind of anger was he burying? Self-destructive—that's what. He was rolling headlong into a good case of self-destructive energy if for no other reason than that's where he wanted to be. The thing was, she was pretty sure he was self-aware, and even more sure that the fact she was a PTSD counselor didn't help the matter, as he was suspicious of her motives.

So be it, she thought. Let him be suspicious, if that's what he wanted. But it wasn't her intention to counsel him even if he asked…conflict of interest and all. Although she did admit that the more she knew him, and the fonder her feelings for him grew, the more difficult it became not to offer a suggestion here and there. And if that's what she was doing she'd have to watch herself more closely. Of course, maybe he was being overly sensitive, too.

What a pair they'd make! One on the offensive and one on the defensive all the time.

So why worry about it so much? Because she cared about him, that's why. She wasn't sure she knew why and she was positive she didn't want to find out. But somewhere, deep down, she felt an affection for the man, and whether or not he liked that, well, too bad. Too damned bad.

Marc kept his eyes on the clock, debating whether or not he wanted to go down and have lunch with Anne. It always seemed like she was pushing him toward PTSD therapy. Was that his own guilt feelings coming through because he knew he could use the help, or was she really pushing as hard as he accused her of? Whatever the case, now she wanted to do it in conjunction with his own therapy modalities. Maybe it was innocent, maybe she didn't mean anything by it, or maybe it was her stubborn belief that she could fix him.

However it played out, he didn't want to be fixed. He'd had enough of that—somebody always knowing what's best for him. Well, he already knew what was best and it wasn't droning on and on about his disability. He'd dealt with that already. Wasn't looking for a repeat, or in Anne's case, someone who meant well but just didn't get it.

In the end, the clock ticked right past the time and he stayed back in his therapy room, wondering if she really had expected him to join her or if her invitation had just been another way of pointing out the merits of a program she thought would benefit him. The hell of it was he was a big advocate of water therapy. He'd spent his fair share of time in the pool because it was good exercise. But when she'd suggested it for him, it had made him feel like a patient again. Put him at a disadvantage with Anne when all he wanted to be was a normal man. Wanted her to see him as a normal man rather than as a cause. Either way, it was a moot point. He hadn't gone, and that was that!

So he worked on through the day, and the day after that, totally avoiding her, even if she was on his mind more than he needed her to be. It had been two days since he'd talked to her other than a cordial greeting in passing, and he desperately wanted something to get his mind off her. Some good, hard physical work.

So after the day was over, and all his patients had been seen by either him or the various therapists who worked in the department, he decided to work it out with a swim. He almost laughed aloud over that one. The cause of their problem was her forcing him back to the water, yet that's exactly where he went anyway when he wanted to let off some steam.

The room containing the swimming pool was stark. It was long and narrow, just the perfect size to fit a lap pool, and one side was lined with wooden benches, while the other was lined with life jackets, various flotation devices and lifesaving equipment. The pool maxed out at six feet deep and there were no diving boards to fancy it up. It was a lap pool, pure and simple. Which was all he needed this evening.

Marc changed into a pair of black trunks, avoided looking at his useless legs, and lowered himself in, then pushed off the side and began to move his way through the water, not like a swimmer who kicked and splashed so much as a graceful fish. All the effort came from his upper body as he went from end to end, then back and forth another two times before he stopped to catch his breath.

"You have a lot of power in your upper body," she whispered in the dimly lit room.

Her presence there startled him, broke his stillness in the water, and he gasped. "What the hell are you doing in here?" he finally growled.

"Looking for you."

"Why?"

"I thought you might like to come over for dinner. It's the least I can do…"

"Not hungry," he grumbled.

"But you will be in due course, especially after the way you've been swimming, like you were running from the gates of hell."

"This is the gates of hell," he snapped. "In case you haven't noticed."

"But you swim so well."

"I swim like I'm disabled."

"If that's how you want to refer to it. But what I just witnessed was a man with a very skilled mastery of his sport—a sport I'd love for him to incorporate into my therapy plan. And if you do consent to it, it would have to be you doing the work because I'm not skilled enough."

"You just don't give up, do you?"

"Not when I think it's a good idea."

"But as you see, I swim. Your little plan isn't going to benefit me."

"Maybe start a swimming team, then. There are competitive teams for people with disabilities all over the country. Perhaps you could develop someone who's good enough to compete, or even compete yourself. Who knows?"

"Because I'm able to take a few laps?"

"Because I have an idea you're good at other sports, too. And one thing translates to another. Besides, you won't know if you don't try."

"That's assuming I want to try. Which I don't."

"So what you're telling me is that if some very gifted athlete ended up in your training program and you saw future potential in him, you wouldn't help him?"

Rather than answering, Marc pushed off the side and swam away from her. But that didn't dissuade her, as she walked along the side of the pool while he swam the length.

"You'd turn your back on him?"

No answer.

"Or better yet, have him transferred to another facility because you don't want to deal with him?"

Again, no answer.

"Why is that, Marc? A good rehab doc would love to find someone with that kind of skill level."

"Then maybe I'm not a good rehab doctor," he shouted. "Maybe I'm a damned lousy rehab doctor and I'm just here biding my time because I've got nothing else to do." He swam to the opposite side of the pool where his wheelchair was sitting and pulled himself out to the poolside. "All I wanted was a few minutes of peace and quiet where I could swim alone. That's not asking too much, is it?"

"Is there ever a time when you don't want to be alone?" she called into the hollow room.

"Is there ever a time when you do?" he responded as he dried himself off with a towel.

"I'll admit I'm social, and I'm not embarrassed by it."

"Well, I'm not and I'm not embarrassed by it, either."

"But don't you ever find yourself in the mood to be around people? And I don't mean your patients."

"Not really. I've chosen my life, and I'm fine with it."

"It chose you, Marc, and you never fought back. You let it consume you."

His side of the pool was quiet for a moment, then she heard the distinct sound of him transferring into his wheelchair. "I don't need your stinking therapy," he said as he wheeled toward the door to the dressing room.

"You need something," she yelled after him. But she was yelling into the dimness as he'd already gone in to change into his clothes. How could a man so independent in one way be so resistant to change in practically every other way? She understood his bitterness, but what she didn't understand was how he'd worked so hard to get himself to a certain point, then quit.

Determined to have the last word in this argument, she crashed through the men's dressing-room doors and stopped when she saw him sliding into his jeans. "You may not need my therapy, but what you do need is to get over yourself. You're self-centered and that leads to a miserable life."

"What if I am?"

"Is that how you really want to be…forever alone? Because I don't believe it, not for one little minute."

He slipped a gray T-shirt on over his perfect torso.

"So what are you proposing to do? Turn me into some Eliza Doolittle…the rain in Spain stays mainly on the plain?"

"No, I'm not proposing anything like that. I'm just saying that you might need help to get over the next hump."

"Provided there's a hump to get over."

Anne headed to the door to the hall. "Oh, there's a hump all right. You know it as well as I do."

"So why do you want to help me?"

"Because someone helped me along the way. Actually, several people did. And I want to pass that on."

"What if I don't want help?"

"What if you do?" she asked, as she entered the hall, leaving Marc all alone in the dressing room. Sure, she was overstepping, and her vow to leave him alone was already blown to bits. But people had overstepped to help her since she'd been as hard-headed as Marc. Once she'd given up the self-pity and all the things that went with it, she'd thought she was done with the whole mess, but that couldn't have been further from the truth.

She'd been moody, too, and bitter. She'd shunned people and been rude. Just like Marc. But a number of her friends had intervened and shown her what she was doing not only to herself but how she was destroying her friendships.

Marc needed that, but he didn't have any friends here. Which was why she'd taken that role upon herself. He needed someone. Besides, she actually liked him. In his less combative moments, when his barriers were down, he was a nice man. Under different circumstances she might have found herself falling for him, but that road was closed both ways. She didn't want it and he sure as heck didn't. Still, there was something about him...

She turned and went back into the dressing room, sitting down on the bench next to him. "Don't live a miserable life, Marc. It's so easy to do. I know because I was there."

"What I don't understand is why you've zeroed in on me as your test subject. Do you always have a project going on and I'm the one for this month?"

"I didn't zero in. Maybe I feel a certain kinship— two doctors starting over in new fields. And in spite of yourself, I do like you. But you're not my project." She reached across and gave him a tender kiss on the lips. Brief, but sizzling. "See, my projects don't ever get that."

He smiled. "You're a confusing woman, Anne Sebastian."

"Not as confusing as you." She stood, went to the hallway door and pushed it open. "Definitely not as confusing as you." Although she did admit to herself she was pretty darned confused by everything about Marc, and that included her growing feelings for him. Love? Hate? Something in between, though admittedly the hands on the clock favored the love setting.

Damn, why did she have to be so confused?

Another evening alone, another bowl of cold cereal. Tonight it wasn't palatable. In fact, he was ready to pour it down the garbage disposal within minutes of fixing it.

"Damn," he said, choking down the first bite, then picking up the glass bowl and hurling it at the wall. Cereal and glass went everywhere, but he didn't care. Right at that moment he didn't care about anything except going to bed and hoping he could sleep until morning. Shortly after crawling in between the sheets, though, he was right back out of bed, in his chair, pacing the floor.

It wasn't like he wanted to spend his life alone. He'd had a girlfriend before he'd been injured. Nice girl. But he'd pushed her away along with everyone else, convinced he wasn't what she wanted anymore. Would she have stayed with him otherwise? Hell, he didn't know, didn't have a clue. He'd pushed too hard, then blamed it on her when she'd left. That had made things easier.

Now he was right back in the same pattern with Anne, pushing her away just as hard as he could. But for different reasons. Sure, he found her attractive. He even enjoyed being around her. But she was getting too close, hitting him in the places that hurt. Knowing him better than he wanted to be known. Hell, she knew things no one was ever supposed to see and all she had to do was guess and she got it right.

If there was ever someone with a proclivity for her job, it was Anne Sebastian. She was a neat little package of compassion and knowledge and intuition all rolled up into one. And that scared him, because her radar was out for him and he had no way of blocking it other than by waging a harder battle than she was. And he wasn't sure he could do that. Wasn't sure he had it in him. Or that he really wanted to. Then it occurred to him. Why not put her to the test? Would Anne leave him alone on the therapy front if he engaged more with her on the social front? Maybe it was worth a try to see just where this thing between them was headed.

With that plan in mind, he returned to bed, but that didn't do him any good, so he got back up, dressed and went back to work to tackle that mound of paperwork. But on his way in, he encountered Anne, who was also on her way back in.

"Patient in crisis," she said as she hurried past him and didn't even hang around long enough to hold the door open for him. When he got inside, though, he heard the crisis—someone down the front hall screaming his head off.

Curious, Marc went that way to see what was going on and found a man standing at the ward clerk's station with a knife, threatening to kill himself. Several staff members surrounded him and Anne was at the front, trying to get everybody there to keep quiet. But to no avail. The buzz was loud, which was causing the patient more agitation.

"OK, clear the area," Marc said. "Everybody! Dr. Sebastian needs *everybody* to clear the area so she can work. So, please, exit this hall."

People began to back away until the only two left were he and Anne. A security guard and a nurse also stayed, but kept their distance.

Anne looked at Marc and gave him a silent thank-you, then turned her attention to her patient. "All right, Rick. Everybody's gone, so why don't you calm down and talk to me now?"

"I'm not talking to anybody. It's not worth the effort anymore. She told me tonight she was leaving me and there's nothing I can do to stop her. So what's the point?"

Very quietly and slowly, Marc rolled backward until he'd come to the nurse, and he ordered a syringe of sedative, a benzodiazepine, to have ready in the event they had a chance to use it. Once it was drawn, he went back to Anne, who was making no headway with her patient.

"He won't budge," she said quietly to Marc.

He pulled out his pocket and showed her the syringe. "Benzodiazepine," he whispered.

She nodded. "If we have the chance."

"We will," he assured her, then began to creep up behind Rick as Anne moved in closer.

"Look, Rick," she said, after she'd moved as close as she believed safe, "maybe I can talk to her to find out what this is about. I could get her on the phone right now."

"Too late," he said despondently. "She wants Rick Junior and Amber to be raised in a sane environment and she said I can't provide that for them. The hell of it is she's right. I can't. So why bother trying to get better when it's already a done deal? She's gone and I've got nothing to get better for."

"Your children are your reason," Anne said. "Even if you can't see them every day, when you get better the courts will work out a custody arrangement and you'll get to see them then. So how do you think they'd feel, knowing they were the reason their dad killed himself? They'd have to go through life with guilt and, trust me, it's something that would never go away. I think they'd understand a war injury such as you've got, but suicide?" She shook her head. "No child should ever have to live with that."

Rick Harper took a look at his knife and dropped it on the floor. Marc moved in to scoop it up before he had a chance to change his mind, while Anne held out her hand to help Rick away from the desk. Once he was out in the open, the nurse and security guard stepped forward and took him by the arms, but he resisted them, pulled back, shoved the nurse to the floor and would have shoved the guard down as well if not for Marc, who lunged from his chair and gave Rick the shot. Rick tried to fight back, but Marc's strength was far greater than Rick's, so he pinned him to the floor until another security guard rushed forward. But by that time either the sedative was kicking in or Rick had totally given up his will to fight, as he caused no resistance when the guard picked him up off the floor and escorted him back to his room.

"You OK?" Anne asked the nurse, who was in a hurry to get up and out of there. "I want you to go next door to the hospital's ER and get looked at. You, too, Marc," she said, her voice clearly showing her authority.

"Don't need to. It was just a scratch," he said, showing her the mark Rick had left on the underside of his right forearm.

It wasn't much, but it was a duty-related injury and there were protocols. "Sure you're fine. You always are. But just this once you're going to follow my order or you won't be coming back to work until you do."

"You're serious!"

"Damned serious," she said. "There was an incident here tonight and you got roughed up. Rehab policy. You get it looked at or you're not cleared to work, and I'm going to make this very clear to you. I won't allow you back to work if you don't follow my orders. I'll go to the board if that's what I have to do. Get it?" Besides that, she cared about him, probably more than she should, and even if he had been injured she doubted he'd tell anyone.

He huffed out an impatient sigh, more for effect than meaning it. "Got it."

"Good. Now, go next door."

He almost smiled as he turned his back to her. He liked her take-charge attitude. It was…sexy and she wore it well. And it was nice to know that she cared about him enough to enforce the rules. Even though it was a waste of time since he was fine, he was flattered by her attention. Still, Anne was clearly in charge, and who was he to dispute that?

Besides, maybe this could be the start of his new plan. Oblige her with the things that didn't involve therapy and maybe she'd forget about the things they fought about. Better yet, once he didn't prove to be such a challenge, maybe she'd forget about him and focus her attention elsewhere. That would be the best outcome, even though he did like having her around, liked seeing her from time to time. Liked her more than he would or should admit. And that was the hard part because he was afraid his feelings were well on their way past liking to something else he just couldn't deal with.

CHAPTER EIGHT

THREE DAYS LATER and all was normal. He was settling into his routine, establishing new departmental policies, establishing rapport with his patients and liking his job as much as any job he could like outside surgery.

All in all, things were going well enough and he was generally pleased. Pleased with his new place with Anne, too. Except for casual greetings, she was staying out of his way, mostly because he was fine as he didn't feel like the threat of PTSD counseling was always stalking him. Although in some odd way he did miss having her around. He especially missed the huskiness of her voice when she asserted herself. It always gave him sort of a tingle.

But this was the way things were meant to be, so he was going to have to get used to them, such as they were. Luckily, the board was allowing him to progress with some changes. They were reluctant, of course, since no one really knew him and he was not a proven expert in the field. But his preliminary ideas made sense. So phase one involved some construction, and a wall was being built to divide the main therapy room in two. That way, people with one form of injury wouldn't be discouraged by progress made by others with different injuries.

He remembered once during his rehab that one of the guys who was a quadriplegic became very belligerent and then inconsolable when a paraplegic who'd spent less time there had made significantly more progress. Of course, you couldn't compare the injuries, but to sit and watch one guy excelling over you, day in and day out…he'd really felt for the guy, which was why he'd set up this new arrangement as his first priority. His therapy was meant to help. Not hinder.

And there were so many more cases similar to that, cases where one patient's progress was actually impeded by another's through nobody's fault other than a lacking facility. The thing was, fighting the fight was hard enough, but watching other outcomes that might progress faster than yours…it could be heartbreaking. So now his therapy departments would have some distinctions in therapy levels. And later there would be private rooms for more individualized attention, or for people who suffered emotional distress. Yes, it was a good plan, and he was proud of it.

"It's coming along," Anne said, greeting him in the hallway.

"I hope we're ready in the next couple of weeks to set it up."

"How are you doing?"

"Is that a professional or a personal question?"

"Is that a professional or a personal comeback?"

Marc laughed. "You're always on guard, aren't you?"

"I was going to say it's the other way around. Look, Hannah is home now, and I'm going over there to fix dinner, so I'll talk to you later."

"Yes, I had an invitation."

"You did?"

"From Hannah herself. She called me about an hour ago and asked if I'd like to join you."

"And you said?"

"That I'd be delighted, of course."

"Of course," she replied.

"Is she up to company?" he asked.

"She's going crazy being home and not having her baby home yet. Having you there will distract her."

"What about you? Will it distract you?"

"No," she lied. "I barely even notice you."

"Now, that's what I call cordial." The corners of his lips turned up slightly, but it was the twinkle in his eyes that gave away his good mood.

Anne arched playful eyebrows and scurried away. It hadn't been her intention to invite Marc to dinner, but it seemed her matchmaking sister had outmaneuvered her. Well, damn it anyway. While she wouldn't exactly be distracted by Marc, she was going to have to be careful around him. Or else her sister and everybody else might get the wrong idea. And it was so, so wrong. Sure, he was handsome. Sure, she liked looking. But more than that? No way.

"Roast chicken, stuffing, whipped potatoes, green beans and cherry pie. Sure looks yummy," Hannah said. "Almost as yummy as Marc."

"Why did you do this?" Anne asked her out of earshot of the men.

"The way you two are off again, on again, someone had to," Hannah quipped as she tasted the potatoes.

"But why you?"

"It's time. You have a thing for him and unless I miss my guess, he has one for you."

"But there are too many fundamental problems in the way. First off, I'm not sure I'm ready."

"Because of Bill? Well, get over him. He was the proverbial one bad seed and you've squished that into the ground."

"Then there's Marc's grumpiness…"

"Versus your stubbornness. Makes you a pretty good match, I'd say."

"And there's his need to be alone."

"Like you didn't go through that yourself? So is it really Marc's disability? Because if it is, get over it. He's one of the good ones who's temporarily going through a bad patch. We all have them, including you!"

Anne shook her head. "It's not his disability. It's more like I can't predict how he's going to be from moment to moment, and that scares me."

"Since when did you want predictability?"

"Since I had Bill."

"Do you have something going on with Marc?" Hannah asked bluntly.

"I don't know. I thought I knew what it should feel like with Bill, but look how that turned out."

"So it is Bill?"

"I'm not going to win with you, am I?"

Hannah smiled and shook her head. "And you don't really want to because you know I'm right about this. You're falling for Marc, even though you're fighting yourself over it."

"I should have stayed home," Anne grumbled, "and argued with myself. At least one side of me would have won."

"What? And miss an evening with Marc? I don't think you'd do that."

"I could walk out that door right now."

"Your loss, Anne, if you do."

"She's quite a cook," Jason commented as he took his second helping of beans. "Anne's the domestic one. Hannah...not so much." He gave his wife's hand a squeeze. "But with a new baby, things might change for a while."

"Don't count on it," Hannah said as she nibbled on a chicken leg. "With a baby at home, I doubt if I'll even notice when you're here."

"I thought you were going to get help," Anne said.

"I don't know yet if I want somebody helping out with the baby or if I want to take a leave for a few years. Now that I've been separated from Annie for a few days, I'm not sure what I'll do. Maybe I'll decide after Mom and Dad are here. Oh, and Jason's parents are coming after ours leave, and his grandmother will be coming after that, so I've got a good two months to decide."

"Maybe Anne will hire out as a domestic," Marc teased. "Cooking, cleaning, that sort of thing."

"I had a husband once who expected that from me. He wanted me to work and he also wanted his meals on the table. It's hard to do when you're a military soldier. He cheated because he said he didn't get enough from me, that all my crazy hours, then going overseas, compromised the sacred estate of marriage."

"He called it 'the sacred estate'?" Marc asked.

Anne shrugged. "He did, which the judge found

hypocritical, considering all the affairs he had while I was busy in the army."

"He didn't have much of a leg to stand on in the divorce proceedings," Hannah said, then immediately started blushing. "I'm sorry. I didn't mean…" Her voice trailed off as she scrambled for the right words.

"That's all right," Marc said. "I don't take offense that easily."

"He has a thick skull," Anne said.

"And you know me well enough to make that judgment?"

Anne straightened her shoulders. "You're like an open book, Marc. Very easy to read."

"You think so, do you?"

"I think so."

"Then give me an example," he said, grinning.

"Your new therapy rooms. Shows empathy. Lots of it, actually. You care for your patients' welfare, and while that might not be expressed in words, you show it in your actions."

"Or efficiency. It doesn't give me more space but it gives me a better use of what's there."

"*Empathy*, dividing your patient classifications. You can call it what you want, but anybody looking in can see it for what it is."

"Or a better way to spend their time in therapy where they don't have to envy someone who's making more progress or pity someone who's not." He smiled. "Shrinks work with emotions, rehab doctors and surgeons employ logic."

"Yeah, right," Anne said. "Empathy is only good for some."

"You said it."

She folded her arms across her chest, barely even noticing goodbyes from Hannah and Jason as they went off to the hospital for their nightly visit to see Annie.

"Why can't you take a compliment?" Anne asked Marc.

"What was a compliment?"

"What I said about what you're doing in your therapy rooms. That's where this all started and you misconstrued…" She looked around and suddenly realized that she and Marc were alone. "See, your arguing ran them off."

"Might have been your arguing."

"I was trying to pay you a compliment." His eyes just sparkled and he was so attractive. She'd admittedly married partially for good looks the first time and he stood in Marc's shadow, lookswise. In fact, Marc was a real head turner, rough edges and all.

"Compliment accepted, but I'm not accepting the blame for your sister running away. That's all on you."

Anne laughed. "I'll accept half the responsibility, not a percentage point more." She really enjoyed this banter and wondered how he'd been before his accident. A lot lighter than he was now, she decided. Damn war, with its casualties! There were too many on all sides. "But you have to accept half the responsibility for cleaning up because I'm pretty sure Hannah doesn't want to come back to it after she's said good-night to the baby."

"You wash, I'll dry. And you can put away since I don't know where anything goes, and I'll clean the table and counters. Deal?"

"Deal," she said. "But I'm wondering now how you're going to wiggle out of your end of the responsibility."

"Let's see…there are so many ways to do that. I

could tell you I'm exhausted, or I've got a patient to see at the hospital, or maybe my muscles are cramping. Want some more?"

"That's plenty," she said, laughing. "And I'll admit you're pretty good at the excuses. I'm never quite that quick on my feet, and once I think of one, the moment has passed."

"You strike me as someone who's very quick on her feet. Like that patient who tried to kill himself the other night. What you said was brilliant."

"And what you did was brave." She filled the sink with sudsy water as Marc took the leftovers and put them in storage bags.

"Not brave. More like a response from my combat training. I've had to pull a guy off the ledge more than once while I was in the battlefield so I've had some practice."

"Why didn't you go into psychiatry?"

"Had no desire to get mixed up in someone else's mental health problems...*at the time*. Of course, things change."

"Just look at the two of us in our different fields."

"But you had a choice. I didn't."

"That's true," she said, as she handed him the first plate to dry. "But you could have landed somewhere in the surgical field if you'd wanted. As an administrator or teacher..."

"Except that wasn't me. I'm a hands-on kind of guy and I like to be closer to my patients than either of those jobs would have allowed me."

"Makes sense."

"So why did you change?" he asked.

"After I was a mess, I just lost heart for general practice. I became intrigued by the whole process of the emotional makeup that in many cases is related to a change in bodily function or perception. I'd come close to being a psychiatrist once before and had changed my mind, so I just changed it back with a little diversion.

"Psychiatry was one of my options, also radiology. I had choices, but radiology never interested me, and as for psychiatry, I don't come equipped with the kind of empathy you need to get involved on the level you do. I want to help, but not with someone's mental health because I've had my own days when I wondered if I was going insane or even going to make it."

"But look at me, Marc. I went down the wrong road and came back to work on that road."

"Because you've got a different emotional makeup than I have." He stacked the plates neatly, one by one, on the counter. "You implode, I explode. That makes a big difference."

Or a good combination, she thought as the last dish was washed, dried and put away. "So, your indentured servitude is over. You're free to go."

"How are you going to get home?"

She sighed intensely. "No car means I call a cab or beg a ride."

"What about a rental car?"

"My insurance should provide one, but so far they haven't. It's a little messed up, but I should get one soon."

"Then I can drive you."

"Sure you don't mind? Because I don't mind waiting here."

"It's late. You've got bags under your eyes. You look like you could use your sleep."

"Are you purposely trying to insult me, or does it come naturally?"

"Maybe a little of both." He hung up the dish towel and headed for the front door. "Or maybe I'm being honest."

"That I look like hell."

"You work too much. It shows on you. So, when was the last time you took a complete day off? One without any work at all?"

"It's hard to do when I have patients who might need me anytime."

"See, that's the thing. Devoted is one thing, but obsessed is another." Marc opened the front door for her, then followed her out. "And trust me when I tell you, I know obsessed."

"Because you are?"

"Because I used to be. Before I was injured. But being a para puts things in a different perspective."

"How so?"

"By necessity, it slows you down, to start with. Gives you a whole lot more time to think and reevaluate your life and what direction you want to go."

"But I'm not convinced you're going in the direction you want."

"It's better than the alternatives. I mean, can you see me teaching medicine to an eager class of first-year med students? It might work for some people but not for me."

"Because you're still too full of life to compromise?" she asked him.

"In my mind I am. And that's not to knock those who teach, because I admire the great teachers of the world past and present. More like it's admitting my weakness.

As a teacher I'd never be great or even good. It's not in my makeup to do that and I'm smart enough to admit it."

He opened the car door for her, then rolled around to the driver's side, which was specially equipped for someone with his condition. "In my mind I'm still driving a sports car and I don't need something with hand controls that accommodates my wheelchair. But in my reality I've made the adjustment, and it's the best of all my choices." He shrugged. "And that's the way it is."

"It's a good choice," she said. "I'm already hearing good things about your work."

He chuckled. "But not about me?"

"You're not easy," she said as he put the car into gear and they moved forward. "Not friendly, most of the time, not even cordial to your colleagues. Good with your patients, though, so I guess that's what counts."

"Being nice to everybody expends a lot of effort I don't want to waste. It's easier to ignore them."

"A smile or a simple nod of the head wastes effort? Aren't you grumpy!" She twisted to look out the window, wondering why she'd agreed to this ride in the first place. She understood that Marc had a gripe with the world, but he dwelt on it every minute of every day and that's what she didn't understand. Why would someone choose to make themselves miserable when help was available? Was he afraid of failure? That if he completely bombed out there was no place else left to go? Had he tried already and failed?

"I don't think that expressing my opinion makes me grumpy. It just makes me...opinionated."

"See, that's the thing. Your opinions are often grumpy."

"But when, exactly, am I grumpy to you? Point it out

to me and I'll stop. In fact, spread the word to the staff. Tell them to call me out if I'm being grumpy to them."

"It's not grumpy so much as standoffish. And you're that way to darned near everybody but your patients."

As they pulled up in front of her house, she paused for a moment before she got out. "I'm the impatient one," she admitted, "and I'm sorry I attributed my attitude to you. But it's not easy seeing your own faults so clearly, is it?"

"It's not a fault. Just part of the personality trait that makes you who you are. Wouldn't want you to change."

"Yet that's what I'm trying to do to you."

"Running into a great big wall of resistance, though, aren't you?" he said, grinning.

"That's true," she said.

"How about we wave the white flag? You don't try to fix me and I won't point out all your own *insufferable* ways."

"I do have a few, don't I?"

"Just a few."

"Then truce it is." She reached out a hand to shake his, but somehow ended up in his arms. "Is this the way you always call a truce?" she asked him.

"I've never called a truce before and this seemed the right way to go about it."

"Maybe it is, but it scares me, Marc."

"Because I'm a para?"

"No. Because I'm not ready, and I don't know how to get myself ready."

"Do you want to?"

She shrugged. "I don't know… Maybe."

"Can't blame a man for trying," he said, gently pushing her away.

"Don't end it yet," she said. "Just give me more time."

"To find even more reasons to be uncertain? No, I don't think so."

She sighed heavily. "I made such a bad mistake once..."

"Which is in your past. Unless you're not completely over him."

"Believe me, I'm over him. But I haven't learned how to move on."

"With a paraplegic to boot."

"Don't make this about you, Marc. It's not!"

"In some way, it's always about me." He smiled regretfully. "I shouldn't have tried. I know better. Now, I think it's time for you to go in. Forgive me for not going in with you, but I'll watch you from here to make sure you get in safely."

She did. And quickly. And felt like kicking the door once she was inside.

The days dragged on one after another and not much changed except the interior factions of his physical therapy workrooms, and they made remarkable progress. He was pleased with their progress, and if things went according to plan, they would be completed within days.

The rehab center was planning on a small reception and dedication, neither of which he cared to be part of. But that went along with the job and maybe it would give him a chance to see Anne, who'd been conspicuously absent from his end of the world since that night in the car. What the hell had he been thinking? Actually, for a moment he'd been a normal man again. Nothing wrong or different about him. Same old urges and attractions. Same old responses. But he was no longer allowed to have these.

No, not him. Had fought honorably in his day. Been discharged honorably when it had been over for him. And been left with so little else to push him along the way. Oh, the help was there if he cared to go out and find it, but what was there to find that hadn't already been found, other than the pieces of pain and heartbreak he kept tucked away as a reminder? But the truth of it was that he'd left so much of himself behind. Until that moment with Anne. Until all the moments with Anne. But he wasn't entitled to those moments, was he? He'd paid his dues, yet that didn't give him back everything, especially the things most essential to life.

Well, she could stay away from him, damn her. Everyone else did, then wondered why he pushed so hard.

The answer was simple. It was easier to push than be pushed. For that one single instant he'd forgotten it, and he didn't blame Anne for her reaction. Wasn't even angry at her. It wasn't her fault. He'd inserted himself into her life in a place where he had no right, and had gotten what he deserved.

"I'm so glad she's home and things are finally settling down for you," Anne said to Hannah, who looked exhausted. Their parents were there, fussing over Hannah and the baby almost incessantly now, and Hannah was enjoying the pampering, happy to have her sister nearby to help when necessary. Or remind their parents they were doting a bit too much.

"There's no settling down with a newborn. Only brief moments of rest. Too brief, too few, and half the time I'm wrestling Mom or Dad for baby time."

"How's Jason handling it?"

"He's doing fine. Splitting the night shift with me and taking as much of it as he can when Mom and Dad will let him. But he needs his sleep, too."

"I can help, too," Anne volunteered. "I can come over some evening and watch her the entire night while you and Jason and Mom and Dad all go out to dinner, then get a good night's rest."

"Would you? I mean, you don't have to, but other than Jason's and our parents and grandparents you're the only one I'd trust with her."

"Just name the night."

"Friday," Hannah said without hesitation.

"Then Friday it is."

"Unless you have a date with that hunk Marc."

"Date? The man is…well, actually, so am I."

"What?"

"Reclusive. We almost had a moment, but we pulled back, and I'm not even sure which one of us did the pulling."

"So there's some attraction there?"

"Some, maybe. Or let's just say there could be. But…" She shook her head. "I don't even know what it is except that he quit just as we were about to get to the good stuff. So did I, though. It's like we've got the chemistry, but we're fighting it."

"Is it his chair?" Hannah asked.

"That's what I keep asking myself and I don't think it is. In fact, I don't even think of it. To me it's just the way he is."

"What chair, what hunk?" Anne's mother cut in. "Are you finally dating someone, dear?"

"No, Mom. Not dating. He doesn't date, and neither do I."

"Why not, especially if he's a hunk?" Joann Sebastian was petite, with glossy brown hair tied back from
her attractive face. Without looking hard, she could
have been mistaken for their older sister.

"So is it your baggage with your first marriage?" she
asked her daughter.

"That's what I'm wondering. I mean, I picked a man
who cheated on me, so what does that say about me?"

"It says you made a mistake. But someday you're
going to have to get over it and move on. We all do
stupid things, Anne. I almost flunked out of nursing
school I was partying so hard, and how many times did
I turn down your father before I finally went out with
him? Probably a dozen." She pulled Anne into her arms
and hugged her. "The best that can be said is that we're
human and, coincidentally, that's the worst that can be
said, too. We all have foibles."

"But some foibles seem bigger by comparison than
others."

Hannah laughed. "Get over yourself. You're taking it
all too seriously. If you care for the man, let him know
and see how it works from there."

"I'm a coward."

"Who could miss out on the best thing ever," her
mother retorted. "Too bad if you do, but don't come
looking for sympathy from me if you don't even try."

"And that's what mothers are for," Anne said despondently as Annie woke up and started crying.

"So much for peace and quiet." Hannah pushed herself off the sofa to head up to take care of her daughter.

"Good thing Auntie Anne is more helpful than her

sister," Anne said on her way up the stairs behind Hannah. "At least I can be called on to do something productive."

"Do something productive and call him," Joann called from downstairs. "Maybe he'll come over here Friday night and help you babysit."

"Quit nagging," Anne said at the top of the stairs. "It'll rub off on the baby."

"And stop moaning and start acting, or it'll become a habit," Hannah said.

The thing was, Hannah and their mom were right. Every word of it. But was she ready to change? That's the part she didn't know and didn't want to think about. Change was difficult. She'd done it once before and she wasn't sure she was up to it again. Wasn't sure at all.

CHAPTER NINE

THE WEEK WENT quickly and she'd had lunch dates with Marc a couple of times, conversations in the hall, even rides back and forth to work before her new car finally arrived.

But tonight she'd decided to do the babysitting alone rather than inviting Marc to join her. She didn't want him to think she was being too pushy, and that seemed pushy. Besides, she was looking forward to a little one-on-one time with her niece.

So Friday hopped up and, true to her word, she went off to babysit for the evening. But when she arrived, Marc's SUV was already there. "What's this about?" she whispered to Hannah. "What's he doing here?"

"Just having a meeting with Jason. He'll be gone in the next few minutes."

Anne's heart skipped a beat. Suddenly a night with Marc looked appealing, but that wasn't to be the case.

"And I'm afraid we're going to have to cancel. Annie has come down with a slight temperature, and we don't want to leave her. I did leave you a voicemail a couple times but I guess you're not listening to your messages."

"Busy day. Is there anything I can do?" The prospect of another Friday evening alone looked bleak. Nowhere to go but home, nothing to do but read. Her life was beginning to close in around her. Of course, that was her choice, wasn't it? She was the one who'd turned herself into a recluse. She was the one who hadn't looked outward for a life.

"Want to go for dinner?" Marc said from behind her. "Since you're not busy and neither am I, I thought maybe we could be not busy together."

"I could be persuaded," she said coyly. Coy? Why was she was suddenly sounding so coy? She was being silly, that's why. She'd wanted something to do and here it was, and she was acting like a schoolgirl out on her first date.

"There's a nice little Italian place over by the park. I've stopped in there a couple of times and it seems good. And it's easily accessible."

"I know the place. It's called Mama Maria's. Great pizza! Since I've finally got my rental car and you've got your SUV, how about I meet you there?"

"How about I drive you there like a real date and we can come back here later and pick up your car?"

"You sure you don't mind?"

"Unless you mind being seen with me."

"That's ridiculous."

"Glad you're going," Hannah said on her way back up the stairs, carrying Annie. "Now I feel better that you two are going on a date."

Anne gave her sister a frown, even though Hannah couldn't see it. "Just an impromptu meeting," Anne insisted.

"That would normally be called a date, except when Anne's involved," Marc replied, "since she makes it quite clear she doesn't date."

"She actually doesn't." Hannah jumped in to defend her twin from the top of the stairs. "Even though we've tried to get her to."

"You know, I'm standing right here," Anne said. "Listening."

"We're not saying anything you don't already know," Hannah replied.

"The thing is, I won't defend myself because I don't want to. We all make our choices." Anne moved toward the door. "And on second thought, to make this seem less datelike, I'll drive myself. See you in ten, Marc."

"Well, have a nice nondate this evening," Hannah called to them.

"They have a nice brick pizza oven."

"I've seen the pizza, even smelled it, and it always seems delicious, but I've never been there," she said.

"Let me guess. You don't generally eat out alone, do you?"

"And you do?" she asked.

"I stop here for a take-out pizza every now and then."

"But you never stay here and eat alone."

"It's a lonely prospect," he admitted. "People look at you…"

"And pity you for being all alone. But the good thing is you vary your diet from cold cereal occasionally."

"Eating is just that. It sustains you. Doesn't matter what it is as long as it gets you by."

She studied him for a moment. "That's a sign of depression, you know."

He chuckled. "I knew you'd pick up on something like that. But the truth is I'm not depressed. I just don't prioritize my eating. Don't care about it one way or the other."

"Then why bother asking me out?"

"Because your plans changed and I was doing the polite thing."

"Then it is a pity meal."

"Maybe a little. But even though we've had lunch and a few hallway conversations, I've missed you this past week and I thought it would be a good way to catch up."

He'd missed her! That caused her heart to clutch. Because she'd missed him, too—those little barbs he was master of, that twinkle in his eyes when he didn't know she was observing him. But it had been easier to stay away than anticipate anything, because she had missed him, and that indicated to her that her feelings for Marc were growing, and shouldn't. And that's just the way it was because she could easily see herself falling for the guy. Or had already fallen.

"It's been a busy week," she replied, and that was no lie. She'd been in a time crunch almost every day, though this had also turned out to be a relief, keeping her away from her confusion over Marc. Not allowing her time to think. "I had four new patients admitted and a setback with one of my regulars. So busy I hardly had time to catch a breath. But I missed you, too."

"Want a personally guided tour of the new physical therapy facilities?" he asked after an hour of pleasantries about med school and childhood and other neutral territories.

"You can get in?"

His answer was to produce a bright, shiny silver key. "You think there's any way they're going to keep me out of there?"

She chuckled. "I suppose there's not."

"Then, that tour?"

"I'd love that tour! It reminds me of being a child and sneaking around on Christmas morning to see where all the packages were hidden."

"Did you find them?"

"We usually found one or two. The rest were hidden in our parents' bedroom, which was strictly off-limits. It was so frustrating knowing they were on the other side of the castle wall yet having no way to get to them. The two of us tried year after year and we never defeated the keepers of the gate."

"My parents' strategy was different. They just put the gifts out and said, 'There, open them now and you'll have nothing to open on Christmas.'"

"Did you ever?"

Marc shook his head. "Nick opened his one year and spent a miserable Christmas morning without anything to open. He never did that again. But me, I always opted for the surprise."

"Except when it's a physical therapy annex and look who's sneaking in."

"I've got to make sure it's coming together correctly. The contractors won't let me in during the day."

"So you sneak in at night. How very...*Christmas* of you."

He laughed. "That *is* what it feels like."

"Then you've done this before?"

"Maybe a couple of times."

She faked a pout. "And I'm not your first accomplice?"

"Oh, you're my first. And if Security catches us I'm telling them you forced me to do it."

"Ah, the gentleman in you comes out." She laughed. "I'll tell them you told me there were Christmas presents in here for me."

"But it's nowhere near Christmas."

"Doesn't matter. He'll be so surprised by my reason I'll have time to escape, which leaves you sitting there holding the bag. Which I doubt has any Christmas presents in it."

"You'd actually let me take the fall for this?"

She nodded and laughed. Marc had it in him to be fun when his guard was down, and she liked that side of him. "So should we go see if we can get in without getting caught?"

The therapy rooms were pretty messy still, with tarps and carpentry scraps and tools everywhere, so they stayed at the doorway and looked in. "Right now it doesn't look half the size it used to be," she said.

"It's not going to be cramped when half the equipment is placed just right in here."

"Didn't you mention space for a couple of private rooms?"

He swallowed hard. "That's going to be a bit more difficult."

"Why?"

"The space I want is already occupied. I'd have to convince someone to move his or her office to another place in the building."

"Her meaning me?"

"It's all just on paper right now."

"You want me to move?" she gasped. "Seriously?"

"Not so much move as rearrange your work facilities."

"And when were you going to spring this on me?"

"When the board budgeted the money."

"Good, because I'll have something to say about that!" she said. "And it won't be in your defense." She smiled. "I'll win, Marc. Just you wait. I'm pretty good at waging battle." And besides, she liked working in his vicinity. It gave her a chance to take quick glances at him from time to time.

"My plan will make sense. You'll see. Your patients can meet anywhere but my patients…they need to stay in the same proximity because of the therapy equipment and the pool."

"So it's OK to inconvenience me and my staff?" She liked sparring with him, liked that connection, especially as neither of them took it personally.

"Not OK, but a better plan. But that's a long way down the road."

"It had better be, because I'm not going anywhere." She folded stubborn arms across her chest. "And I'm not changing my mind. Where I am suits me perfectly."

"In time you'll see the beauty of it, when I can figure out…"

"What? Where to put me?"

"Something like that. But it's not as drastic as it seems. Trust me."

Well, he had another think coming if he thought he could out-stubborn her into moving, because it wasn't going to happen. His warning gave her a chance to come up with her own defensive plan for when the time came. Suddenly, Anne was smiling. Nope, he didn't know how stubborn she could be.

"What's that about?" he asked.

"Only a plan of my own. You wait and see, Dr. Rousseau. You're not the only who can make plans around here."

"Well, I've got a plan."

"Should I trust you?"

"Of course not. But I'll tell you anyway. I'm going to go take a swim before I go home. Want to come take a swim with me?"

"I would, except I don't have a suit."

"No one's there at night. The pool's strictly off-limits. I can dim the lights, or do the gentlemanly thing and turn my head, even though I'm a doctor and I've seen naked bodies before."

"Ah, but this naked body isn't one of your patients."

"What happened to my brave little Christmas girl?"

"She was fully dressed when she was sneaking around, looking for gifts."

He shrugged. "Well, it's up to you. I'm going to get a swim in tonight, and you're welcome to bring your tired, achy muscles along and join me. Or watch me. Or neither."

He wheeled off toward the pool locker room and changed into trunks, while she stayed back in the hall, wondering if she should add a little adventure to her life. She was getting pretty stagnant, after all. She either worked or did something for her sister. That was it.

Anne thought of all the men and women she'd treated—the ones she'd helped, the ones she hadn't been able to help. Such bravery. And here she was, afraid to take a tiny step. Batting at the tears in her eyes, she pushed through the door to the pool, dimmed the lights, stripped down to her scant underwear and slipped in— they would dry quickly enough in the hand driers in the changing room.

"Change of heart?" Marc asked from the shadows.

But Anne didn't hear. She was swimming away her demons with one hard stroke after another. Covering the length of the pool with remarkable speed.

"You have a lot of grace in the water," he said, not even coming close to catching her.

"So do you, and strength, if you want to use it. But you'd rather waste your time, wouldn't you? Play like you're giving them something back rather than get really invested."

"You came in here to fight me about a swim team?"

"No, I came here to forget you, forget me, forget all of it." She swam up to the corner and huddled there awhile to catch her breath. And Marc allowed her all the space she needed.

"Look, I'm sorry," she said after a little while, when she could hear that he'd stopped swimming. "It's just that you've got so much potential and you're wasting it. So many people could benefit from your athleticism, but that's where you'd have to go beyond the call of duty and really put yourself out there."

"Didn't I already do that once?"

"And you want to stop living after that? See, what I don't get is the way you're wasting your potential, as well as the potential of others. You've got a long life ahead of you, Marc, and you act like your injury ended it then and there. But that's not the case."

"This is why I swim alone at night. So no one will bother me."

"Including your conscience?"

"My conscience is just fine, thank you very much!"

"Everything about you is fine except your conscience."

"Hey, I have an idea. Let's swim!"

Anne laughed. "Now I'll never know who won that round."

"Let's call it a draw." He swam up to her and splashed a little water in her face. "Race you to the end of the pool."

With that, she was in for the swim of her life, and discovered just how formidable he was in the pool as he outswam her by nearly half a length, then turned round and came back to meet her. She was laughing when he caught up to her...laughing and bobbing up and down in the water. "You're seriously good," she said, gasping for breath.

"Is that going to raise the old argument again?"

"Just sayin', Marc..."

"I'm good, I should coach."

"See. Even you know it."

"You don't give up, do you?"

"I do, but not easily."

He chuckled. "Well, neither do I."

"So I've noticed."

"Ready for another race to the end?"

"Knowing full well you'll beat me? I think I'd rather do this more leisurely while you swim circles around me."

She drifted close to him on her way to the edge of the pool...so close their bodies came into intimate contact, and the next thing she knew his arms were around her, hers were around him, and they were kissing, and it wasn't a friendly little peck on the cheek or lips like before but a full-out kiss where tongues probed and bodies tightened. If she'd ever had any doubt he could function as a man all the way, this kiss told her otherwise as the water pulsated, driving his pelvis into hers.

Had they not been in a public place, suits would have been shed quickly, but they weren't. As they were reminded when the full lights came on. "Who's there?" a voice boomed out.

Their heads popped up in the water and Marc moved quickly and protectively to block the guard's view of Anne, partially naked now, her remaining underwear having gone particularly transparent.

"Oh, Doc Rousseau, Doc Sebastian, I didn't know… nobody told me." It was obvious that the security guard was quite flummoxed as he backed out of the pool room, his mind probably full of things that had never happened, but could have. Things both Anne and Marc wanted.

Anne was embarrassed, and swam straight for the corner of the pool for protection, while Marc had a good laugh as he went looking for her bra, which had somehow gone adrift in the heat of the moment. "Bet it will be rumored throughout the rehab center in five minutes. It'll probably take seven for it to get next door to the hospital."

"Five," she said, shaking. "Why so optimistic?"

"To cheer you up."

"I don't need cheering up. I need a towel."

Marc pulled one off a stack on the side of the pool and gave it to her. "Would we have?" he asked as he pulled himself up and out of the water.

"In that moment, maybe. But it was only that moment. Don't get it confused with any other moment because we got carried away and that's all it was." She climbed out of the pool, knowing full well she was on display in the glare of the overhead lights, but as she wrapped the towel around herself and stood up she noticed he was doing the courteous thing by not overtly staring. For which she was grateful and maybe even a little disappointed. "Give me ten minutes," she said, then grabbed up her clothes and scooted into the women's locker room.

When she got there, she simply stood with her back to the wall for a few minutes, wondering what had gotten into her. She'd certainly never done anything like that before and it horrified her to think she was capable of doing it with so little provocation.

Back in the men's locker room, Marc was smiling and whistling a peppy tune.

It had been two days since their encounter in the pool and while they'd exchanged quick glances and hurried hellos in the hall, that's as far as it had gone. Truth was, he'd gone too far and he wasn't happy with himself about it as Anne was clearly conflicted about what she wanted. So he shouldn't have pushed her. But what if they'd gone on to where they'd most certainly been headed? Then what? It would have been all or nothing, and Anne wasn't that kind of girl. She needed courting, slowly, deliberately. Anything else was below her. And here he'd probably come off looking like some randy beggar who was only looking for sex.

"Could have been worse, I suppose," Anne said, setting herself down next to Marc, who was taking some private time on the mats to do push-ups.

"We're talking now?"

"We never weren't talking. That was just your imagination."

"Were you processing what happened?"

"Over my embarrassment at being caught almost in the act? Absolutely, yes. But the strange thing is nobody's said a word to me. Or teased me. It's like nobody knows."

"I hope for your sake that's true, but I wouldn't count on it. I mean, what are they going to say? Done anyone in the pool lately, Anne?"

She laughed. "Maybe you're right. But I can still be embarrassed if I want to be."

"You did have a good time, didn't you?"

"Yes," she admitted. "Except for that whole public place situation, and I still can't believe I gave in to that."

"Well, you did. I was there."

"Sometimes you can't fight human nature, I guess."

"I've spent these past couple of days avoiding it," he said.

"By avoiding me. I know."

"I decided to let you have your space to work it out."

"And I appreciate that."

"So did you?"

"What? Get it worked out? It was simple. We got stopped from doing something we wanted in that moment. It's not a big deal."

"But it is to you, Anne. No matter what you say, I can sense that. Still see it in the blush in your cheeks."

"OK, it was. I've spent the last couple of days kicking myself. Then I let it go as much as I can. I'm good at that—letting go of the things that don't need to be hung onto. It's something I do in my counseling—teaching men and women to prioritize."

"So I've been worrying over something you dropped to the bottom of your priority list?"

"That about sums it up. What happened happened. End of story. Anyway, I'm going to a PTSD symposium down in downtown Chicago next weekend. I heard Jason's mandating you go as well. I thought you might like to come with me and sit in on some of the latest techniques, since the majority of your patients do suffer from it. Separate rooms. Hands-off policy!"

"Is this another attempt to get me to give in and get therapy?"

"Nope. It's something that will allow you to further your education on the subject. That's all. No hidden motives."

"Then thanks but, no, thanks."

"Even though Jason's requiring it?"

"Think I'll tell Jason I'm scheduled off all next weekend and he can't dictate my time off."

"What if I asked you to go as a favor?"

"Why?"

"Chicago for one is so…big. I don't like the idea of going alone, and since you have to go…"

"What good will I do you?" he asked, trying to avoid her gaze as she watched him exercise.

"You'll be company. I'll stop short of saying good company because I don't know if you will be, but I'm betting you can put on your good company face for a couple of days if you want to."

"So you know I might be bad company, yet you ask me?" Rather than annoying him, that made him laugh.

She shrugged, then laughed, too. "I think the odds are highly in my favor."

"You really want me to go, don't you?"

"It would be nice." She shifted backward to the edge of the mat as he rolled over and sat up.

"What do you want from me, Anne? Really? What do you want?"

"Do you like me?" she asked.

"What if I do?"

"Do you like me more than a little?"

"Why would I let myself go and do that?"

She shrugged. "Maybe because, in spite of your ways, I like you and I think you're worth the gamble."

"You consider me a gamble?" He scooted over to the edge of the mat table and transferred himself back into his chair.

"Well. You do have your moods."

"Which you attribute to PTSD!"

"Partially. But I think some of it's just plain discontent. You used to be more active and your limitations make you grumpy."

"If you mean I'd rather be operating, you're right. I would be."

"But that's not going to happen."

"I know that, but I don't have to like it."

"But you don't have to hate it, either."

He let out an exasperated breath. "So what do I get out of this weekend if I decide to go get some education I don't want."

"Time away. I could say with a charming companion, but I suppose charming is in the eye of the beholder and half the time I think I annoy you. Oh, and no repeat of the swimming-pool incident. That was then, now it's the aftermath of an incident." She blushed. "One not to be repeated."

"You're blowing things way out of proportion."

"And we went too far," she said awkwardly. "That

pool's to be used for therapy, not for what we were doing."

"We didn't do anything, Anne."

She glanced up at him for a moment. "And we won't. So let's make this trip to the city as amicable as we can. OK?"

"Couldn't you have requested another doctor to go with you?"

"I could have, but Jason wanted you."

"And this is where I tell you I'm flattered?"

"Yes, actually, it is. Oh, then you accept, if not graciously, then fake a pleasantry."

"You're that sure of yourself, aren't you?"

"Yes, because we're still arguing about it and you haven't completely told me no."

He scowled at her for a moment, but the twinkle in his eyes shone through. "Tell me, what are my perks, if I accept?"

"All expenses paid. Room with a view."

"Of what?"

"The skyline."

"Doesn't sound like that many perks to me."

"Best I can do. Maybe breakfast for one in bed— cold cereal."

"Well, I suppose it beats doing paperwork, doesn't it?"

Anne laughed. "You're not happy if you don't have something to complain about, are you? Looking at the trip as the lesser of two evils."

"One of the fundamental joys of my life."

"Anyway, we'll drive down Friday night and come home Sunday night. Pack casually, except for one suit for the reception on Saturday night."

"You're assuming I'm coming."

"I'm assuming you're coming. Now, I think I'm going to go get lunch. Care to join me?"

Marc declined, citing a patient appointment, then wheeled away, leaving her standing there watching him go. So what had convinced her to want him to come along? She wasn't sure except that the more she was around him, the more she liked him. His grouchiness or stubbornness or whatever you wanted to call it was a wall, and while she didn't know how she was going to do it, she was going to kick it down one way or another.

CHAPTER TEN

THE DRIVE INTO the heart of Chicago was blessedly short and quiet. They listened to music and, of course, they couldn't agree on what they wanted. She was in a classical mood, he was all up for blues and jazz. They stopped for dinner. He wanted tacos, she wanted Italian. So they agreed to disagree and finally found a compromise, talking about various patients.

It wasn't what he'd expected, but it was nice to get away. Not that he intended on attending much of the symposium with her. That would be an admission that she was right about him, that a little head-shrinking was all he needed. That's what this weekend was about and he knew it. Something to show him the error of his ways.

Well, she could show all she wanted, but he hadn't told her yet that he was going to spend at least half the time playing tourist. He'd decided to let that wait until the symposium actually started in the morning. Then he was going to Navy Pier while she sat in a stuffy room, listening to a stuffy lecture. Such was life…

The room was nice, and true to her promise, she gave him the one with the view of the skyline. Not that he was going to accept it, but he did like teasing her, liked goading her into decisions and actions she might not otherwise be drawn into. Such as being her plus one at the symposium. He'd been surprised when she'd asked him, but the more he'd argued against it, the harder she'd argued for it, and he liked that. Liked that drive in her.

And he hadn't really minded the compromise of Mozart on the drive since she'd been the one doing the driving. Personally, he'd only asked for tacos because she'd mentioned Italian first. Italian, or anything not cooked in the rehab's kitchen would have been fine. But she always expected an argument from him and he enjoyed giving it.

Of course, there was that incident in the pool, and that had twisted things up in his mind. Suppose it had been more for her? Suppose she was falling for him? Then what? How could he extricate himself from the situation without hurting her? Because he truly had no intention of hurting Anne. Fact was, if circumstances had been different he'd have been going after her as hard and as fast as he could. But those days were behind him now. He didn't get to go after the ladies because he couldn't discern what was genuine and what was pity.

With Anne, though, he didn't think he saw pity there. At least, if he did, he didn't recognize it as such. From the first day, she'd treated him like she did anybody else. No kid gloves. No tiptoeing around him. No guarding words. He liked that…liked it a lot. Still, there was nowhere this could go, no place where it could ever work out, because someone like Anne needed a man and not what was left of one. Forever alone. That was his motto now, and he had to live by it or else risk getting hurt.

"Nice view," he said, rolling in through the double doors.

"I'm across the hall with the view of the…roof and air-conditioning."

"I'll take that one since I'm not a gazer. It doesn't matter where I sleep."

"Doesn't matter where I sleep, either, so you get the view because I promised."

"But I insist."

"And I uninsist."

He chuckled. "So this is what our arguing boils down to? You say to-*may*-to, I say to-*mah*-to?"

"You're here, you stay."

"Or I can…" He wheeled out the door to the hall and crossed over to the other room. "Stay here."

"You're incorrigible, Marc! And I bet you don't intend on going to one of the lectures, do you?"

"I saw a couple on mind-body healing that might be good."

"Really? Because I'm sitting on one of the panels."

"Saw that, too." She was genuinely pleased he would attend her panel discussion. "Any other sessions?"

"Maybe one or two. No promises."

"But you'll escort me to the reception."

"I promised, and I don't break my promises." He smiled. "And I'm looking forward to it."

"Are you really?"

"I wish you trusted me more."

"It's hard to tell when you're serious and when you're…" She shrugged. "I just never know, Marc. And I know that's my fault as well as yours."

"Well, we've got a whole weekend ahead of us. Let's both try a little harder."

"Then I'll be the first to start off by taking the room

with the view," she said, tossing her bag on the king-size bed.

The entire room was elegant, and even Marc noticed that. Reproduction Victorian furniture, fresh flowers, a bottle of welcome champagne on ice.

"Do you drink?" he asked seriously.

"I'd never turn down a lovely glass of champagne. Care to pop the cork and do the pouring?"

Marc obliged, and as they clinked glasses he offered a toast. "Here's to a nice weekend with a friend."

"With a friend," she repeated, wondering if he really was a friend. She wanted him to be, even though it was difficult.

"So why champagne and not a beer?"

"Champagne's more elegant. I suppose a night in a nice room isn't beerworthy."

"It is among friends who are staying across the hall from each other."

"Then maybe there'll be beer in yours. At least, in the minifridge."

"What say we do this? Cork up the champagne, go find a pub and have a beer."

She smiled. "And that will make us both happy. I sure do like compromises."

"So what's going to happen to the essence of what's us, going from so opinionated to blending our opinions?" he asked. "If that's possible."

"Anything's possible. This is Chicago, after all. It's a city that's supposed to make you happy and fill you with possibilities. Just look at the view." She pulled back the curtains and exposed the most magnificent view of lights from buildings of all heights and sizes,

as far as the eye could see. "Have you ever seen anything like it?"

"No, I haven't." He rolled up beside her to look, and
for a moment he was tempted to take her hand. But he
stopped himself by just brushing the back of her hand
with his, then backed away. The last thing he needed
was a romantic room with a romantic view. Now he
wished to God he hadn't come, because this was going
to be a lot tougher than he'd counted on, being so near
her and yet so far away.

"I know this place. It's a little blues club about three
blocks from here," she said. "Since you spent the whole
trip listening to my classical music, would you like to go
down there for an hour or so and see what's playing?"

"Can't," he said, stiffening as he backed away even
more. This was almost too personal. "I need my rest."

"But I thought… I mean… It's still early, and I know
you work longer shifts than this back home."

"The trip tired me out more than I thought it would
and it's just now catching up with me." He saw that she
looked perplexed, maybe even a little hurt, but there
was nothing he could do to stop it. Getting any more
involved with Anne was only going to lead to problems
he couldn't control. Or fix.

"Want anything from room service?" she asked, the
look on her face showing clear letdown.

"I'm fine."

"Was it something I said?" she asked.

"Nothing you said or did. It's just me, feeling tired,
like I said." Lies, every word of it. She made him nervous. What he wanted from her made him more nervous and he just couldn't take it that far. Right now, his
disability might not mean much to her, but what about

years from now, or even months from now? Would it encumber her or hold her back? Could they even settle into a normal life, or would she end up resenting him? No, he just couldn't risk it.

"I just wanted you to enjoy the weekend," she said, backing away from the window and closing the curtains. "That's all this was supposed to be about. Why I suggested to Jason that he—"

"You suggested dragging me to the symposium in the hope that I'd learn something I'd recognize in myself? Which I already do." That he was a lousy liar.

"I didn't think for a minute you'd go to most of the symposium. Just to the reception tomorrow night. And, no, my intention isn't to parade you around like my pet puppy so people can ooh and aww me and tell me what a good girl I am for bringing the disabled man. I just didn't want to come alone. I get tired of always going alone, which is the way my life has been ever since I came back from Afghanistan. The thing is, Marc, I can be honest with myself. I've had a lot of practice and it works."

"Then if you're being so honest, are you attracted to me?" He hadn't meant to ask that question aloud, but it was out there now and he couldn't take it back.

"I am," she said, as heat rose in her cheeks.

"And do you expect me to be attracted in return?"

"Are you?" she asked.

"I need to know why," he asked.

"Are you?" she persisted.

"Tell me why, Anne. Why me? Is it because you want to be a martyr to a cause again? That you can't trust another man after what the first one did to you?" He slapped the wheels of his chair. "Don't you think this will get in the way eventually? After the novelty of dating the disabled man wears off?"

She stepped forward and slapped him. "You bastard," she hissed, then grabbed his bag and tossed it into the hall. "So much for calling a truce," she said as she stepped back.

"If there was ever a way to mess up a relationship, that's it," he said to the bathroom mirror minutes later as he surveyed the red mark she'd left. And, yes, he'd deserved it because, damn it, he *was* attracted to her and those were words that should have been easy to say. All she'd wanted had been the truth and all he'd given her had been another brick in his ever-growing wall.

Talk about being a drama queen. She really wanted to go and apologize to Marc for slapping him, but half of her was convinced he'd deserved it. The other half thought he deserved it, too, but she was being over-reactionary about the whole situation. Either way, she wasn't ready to confront him yet. Didn't want to see him or talk to him. Didn't want to be anywhere near him. Of course, he'd made it quite clear he didn't return any type of feelings toward her. That was a mighty sore vein to open just after she'd finally admitted to herself, and to him, that she was attracted to him.

Well, now he knew and he could do anything with that information he wanted. In fact, now she wished he'd just go home and leave her to her weekend. It was going to be tough trying to glean any information from the workshops when all she could do was play out the last scene in her mind.

"Anne," he called as he knocked on the door. "I think we should talk."

Anne didn't answer for a minute, then finally replied, "I think we've said everything that needs to be said."

"I want to apologize."

"For being truthful? No apologies necessary."

"But I wasn't being truthful... There was no excuse for that."

"What you said was the truth. I don't trust men because of what he did to me. And I'm not in the mood to discuss it."

"Would you be willing to talk if I told you that you're the most drop-dead gorgeous woman I've ever met?"

"Too little, too late. I don't need to be placated. Your first opinion, or shall we call it your lack of opinion, said it all. You don't get a do-over."

"Open the door."

"No! Now go away, leave me alone. I'm not in the mood to argue."

"You're only going to have to face me in the morning, or the day after that."

"I will when it's necessary."

"Are you sure—"

"Leave me alone, Marc," she said wearily. "Please, just leave me alone."

After that, not another word was spoken, and the frigid barrier between them remained up until daylight poked in through the gap in the curtains.

In her suite, Anne had barely slept. In his room, Marc was no better off. Sure, he was falling for her, and in his semi-dream state they'd met when he could still walk and their romance was epic. But when he cleared his head he knew that while he dreamed the dream, he lived the nightmare.

By the time he'd showered and shaved, and knocked

on her door, Anne was gone. She did leave a note saying the reception was at six followed by the welcome banquet, but that he didn't have to attend either one if he didn't want to. She'd also left him a train schedule in case he wanted to go home early.

Talk about being blunt! He actually chuckled. That was one of the reasons he cared so much for her—her honesty. She was a straight shooter, unlike anyone he'd ever known. And he fully intended to go to that reception as her escort, whether or not she liked it. Then maybe somewhere in the evening they could talk, try to straighten things out.

The day rolled past pretty quickly for Anne as she went from lecture to lecture. Then at five she dashed up to her room to take a quick shower and get herself ready for the evening's festivities. She'd purposely kept Marc out of her mind until these past few minutes, when she'd wondered if she'd find him in his room or if he'd actually gone home as she'd hinted he do. As it turned out, he was waiting for her. Dressed in charcoal-gray slacks and a navy blazer, he was what writers referred to as breathtakingly handsome, and she did have to admit that even though he'd thoroughly embarrassed her, she still found him to be the most attractive man she'd ever set eyes on.

"So you're coming?" she asked as she rushed past him to the elevator.

"I was invited. Is the invitation still good?"

"Of course it is," she said, stopping at the door to wait, when what she really wanted to do was take the stairs to run away from him. "And about last night—"

"Last night was last night." Grinning, he rubbed his jaw. "Although I must say you pack quite a punch."

"I was angry."

"And what I said, or didn't say, was uncalled for. I'm sorry, Anne. I didn't mean to hurt you the way I did. I took a cheap shot, and I shouldn't have. Shouldn't have put you on the spot, either."

She shrugged. "No big deal."

"Except it was a big deal. And I was rude."

"Apology accepted."

"If you'd rather I don't go with you this evening, I'd understand."

"If you'd asked me earlier, I'd have said I prefer that you go home. But since you didn't, and since we've made up for now, I'm glad you stayed." She stepped into the elevator first, her face flushed, her hands shaking. This was a man to whom she'd admitted she had feelings, but nowhere in his apology had he admitted the same. Well, better to face her shame and get on with it rather than keep dwelling on it. Otherwise the rest of her trip was going to be miserable. Maybe even her job.

Nope, she'd made the admission freely and now it was time to get past it.

Their walk to the lobby where the reception was being held was a long, quiet one. Even in the elevator, where people were chatting, Anne and Marc were quiet. But once they got to the reception and introductions were made, conversation started to flow. In fact, Marc ran into a couple of old buddies, which made the evening even more pleasant for him.

By the time the dinner was over, he was ready to be out of his suit almost as much as Anne was ready to be out of her high heels. "Care to go for a walk?" he asked, once they were back in his room. "I thought that since it's still early we could go to the Willis Tower observation deck and spend a few minutes…observing."

"Can I change my clothes first, get into some jeans and walking shoes? These symposiums are fun, but there's nothing like relaxing at the end of the day."

"Sounds like a plan."

So ten minutes later they met at her door and went to the elevator. Got on and walked the three blocks to their destination, with Anne talking the whole time about various aspects of PTSD that had been discussed during that day's lectures. Luckily, the line to the observation deck was short, so the wait was only a few minutes. Once at the top, they found it to be a breezy splendor, being able to see miles and miles of lights in any direction.

"Can you believe that as many times as I've been to downtown Chicago, I've never once come up here," she said, perched at the edge of the enclosed bannister. "It's amazing."

"Well, this is my first time playing tourist in Chicago, too, and I'm enjoying it. I took in Navy Pier today, and tomorrow I might try to squeeze in the Aquarium or the Institute of Science and Industry *after* your panel discussion."

"It's boring stuff if you're not interested in PTSD."

"Nothing about you is boring," he admitted. "In fact, at the risk of another rumble I'd say you're pretty interesting."

"Me, interesting?"

"Well, I've already admitted you're beautiful. And that night in the pool showed how much I'm attracted to you."

"But those are all physical attributes. You never answered—"

"Yes. The answer is yes! But that's as far as it goes. I don't get involved."

"Well, this time I'm going to avert the argument and say there's so much to do here." She moved over to another side of the observation deck. "So many places to go, so many places to see." She looked down at Marc. "I'm glad you came along."

"More like you duct taped and dragged me."

She laughed. "That, too."

"But it was worth the fight."

Anne was doing her best to stifle a yawn but it did no good. She was exhausted from a long day, on top of a lack of sleep the night before. All she really wanted to do now was go back to her room and relax for a little while, then go to bed. "Do you mind if we call it an evening?" she asked, as another yawn overtook her. "I'm really tired and—"

"Want me to give you a lift?" he asked, his eyes twinkling.

"A lift?"

"In my chair?"

"Don't offer what you don't intend to go through with, because it sounds tempting. And as tired as I am…"

"I'm willing," he said.

"But I'm not. And how silly would that look anyway?"

"No sillier than you staggering into buildings because you're so tired."

"Thanks, but I'll walk."

"Offer stands."

"If you see me stagger into a building, just grab me, OK? I don't want to hurt any innocent buildings in my delirium."

As the two walked back to their rooms, a cool breeze blew from the buildings to the alleys and sent a shiver up Anne's spine. Without giving it a thought, Marc reached out and took hold of her hand, and they walked as any lovers would along the street, looking in windows, stopping to admire a sight that particularly interested them, or simply sky-gazing. It was beautiful early autumn, too, when the trees still clung ferociously to their leaves but the briskness swirled all around them.

Anne, who was acutely aware of Marc's calloused hand in hers, liked the strong feeling of it, and she was in no hurry to get back to the hotel. But three blocks was all she was allowed, and as they entered the lobby they dropped hands when greeted by a swarm of colleagues on their way out for some late-night carousing. Invitations were extended to join them, but Anne declined with a yawn and followed Marc to the elevator. Twenty-two floors later their evening was over. No more walking, no more holding hands. No more nothing. They entered their own little sanctuaries and that was it.

But it was a very nice way to end the evening. Except that ten minutes later, after she was in her grungy old nightshirt with her hair tied up and her face glopped with moisturizer, a knock on her door startled her.

"Who's there?" she called.

"Strangers bearing gifts."

Oh, no! She looked horrible. But there wasn't time to fix herself up, so, wiping off the face cream on her way

to the door, she did open it a crack. And there he was
with chocolate-covered strawberries and beer.

"It's lovely!" Anne exclaimed as she sank down into
the soft cushions of the sofa in the living room and
leaned her head back on the embroidered pillow. "But
I apologize for the way I look."

"Quite the contrary. I owed you more than an apology," he said, taking his place next to her.

"We all make mistakes and say things we don't
mean."

"You're too gracious," he said, bending forward to
pick up a strawberry. Then he held it to her lips. "And
I'm an ass."

"You are," she said, nibbling the first bite from between his finger and thumb. It was a beautiful red berry,
all ripe and plump, dipped in chocolate and drizzled
with white chocolate. And she really would have liked
to take it from him much less gracefully, but Marc was
making a sweet effort to put his rough edges behind
him. So she took her bite and watched him devour the
rest. They were like a couple who knew the subtle ins
and outs of courting when, truth was, she'd never been
wooed, never been courted in all her life. First marriage included.

"Why are you doing this?" she finally asked Marc
after she'd shared another of the delicious strawberries.
"And don't tell me it's an extension to your apology, because I'd already forgiven you."

"Maybe it's because I wanted to. It seemed like…like
it was the right thing to do after all you've done for me."

"So it's payback?" Truthfully, she was a little hurt
by that.

"Not payback. I'm really awkward in situations

like this. Before my accident I wasn't a romantic. I've had plenty of girlfriends over the years, but they were merely situations. And while I didn't use them, per se, I never had any intention of getting involved, either. A long time ago, I promised myself I'd be a player until all my play ran out. So that's how I was living it. And, believe me, none of them ever warranted strawberries.

"But things changed. I changed when I went to Afghanistan and saw the conditions there. Some of the women…" He cringed. "They had to be so strong to survive. That's when I knew my life was headed in the wrong direction, that I had to change, and even before I was injured I vowed to do things differently once I was out of there. As luck would have it, the course my life would take became decided for me."

"But you're still at war with yourself."

"Over the loss. Over my lack of ability to change my life for myself. I never got the opportunity. Everything was taken away from me and I didn't have any control." He handed her a bottle of beer. "Here's to better times." He clinked his bottle to hers in a toast. "For both of us."

"Better times," she repeated, feeling so tired and yet so exhilarated. Her body wanted to snuggle into his arms and drift off, but her mind didn't want to miss a minute of his conversation. Didn't want to miss a minute of this closeness. "And just for the record, I am attracted to you. I meant it when I said it last night."

"You don't know what you're saying," he said, without pulling back from her.

"I always know what I'm saying, Marc. I see through your armored exterior and I like what's underneath. You're a good doctor, you care, and you're so darned romantic it's making my head swim. So, is this a seduction?"

He was taken aback by her straightforwardness. "It might have been at one time."

"But not now?" she coaxed, puckering her lips into a pout.

"Do you want to be seduced?"

"Do you want to seduce me?" she asked.

"Something tells me I'm the one who's being seduced."

"It's a beautiful night, we have strawberries, my bed is comfortable. So is the sofa, for what it's worth. So why not?"

"I haven't been with a woman since… I mean I tried once, but…" He shrugged.

She put her fingers to his lips to silence him. "Those kinds of things don't matter and she must have been the wrong woman."

He bent his head low to her ear and whispered, "Just so you know, I can function as a man."

Her eyes twinkled. "I never had any doubt about that."

CHAPTER ELEVEN

SHE REALLY WANTED to linger in bed this morning, skip the first lecture or two and stay there with Marc until it was time for her panel, but the hospital was paying her way and she knew it was her obligation to attend the workshops. So, reluctantly, Anne dragged herself from the bed and barely made it to the bathroom she was so weak-kneed.

To say he was a skillful lover was underestimating it. Marc had been masterful in every way, and she desperately wished they could spend one more night there, but noon was checkout time and there was no disputing the fact that they were both scheduled to work tomorrow.

Too bad she couldn't have it both ways. But duty did call and she was nothing if not a slave to the things that had to be done.

Surely there would be another time, another place for Marc and her, though. She hoped so, anyway, because he'd made her feel like a…a princess. And normally one-night stands didn't get the kind of detail she'd gotten. At least she didn't think so as she'd never had a one-night stand before. In fact, the only man she'd ever had before Marc had been her husband, who hadn't been attentive, who hadn't cared about her pleasure, who'd done nothing with flair the way Marc had.

"It's time to get up," she whispered to Marc, after she'd showered and slipped into her black silk bra and panties. "You've got to check out for us in a few hours and I've got a couple of morning lectures to sit in on before my panel."

"Boring lectures," he said, patting the bed beside him.

"Mandatory lectures."

"Mandated by whom?"

"Well, not really mandated, but Jason didn't send me here to play. I'm supposed to—"

"To what? Ignore the man in your bed? The man who wants one more hour?"

"I can't," she protested.

"Who's to know? Nobody takes attendance at these seminars."

"I'll know."

"So what are you going to do? Go back and confess to Jason that you skipped a lecture because you decided to hang back and make love with me?"

"I'd like to hang back, but—"

"Be your own woman, Anne. Do what you want to do for a change, and not what someone else expects from you."

She looked down at him, studied the lines of him that were clearly visible beneath the sheet, then kicked herself for being tempted. But, God help her, she was. She wanted to feel his hands on her body again, exploring, bringing her to climax after climax. Knowing just when to start and stop, just where to touch, to kiss, to caress.

Mercy, was he good. So good she was sliding out

of her bra before she even knew what she was doing and climbing back in the bed with him. One more time was what she promised herself, but with Marc there was never just one more time. And as she dipped her head below the sheets to give him the same pleasure he'd given her, she knew she was already spoiled for life. Marc had bared his all to her and an entire lifetime wouldn't be enough to take it all in.

"I really do have to catch the last lecture before my panel, then we have a luncheon and after that we can go to the museum, then it's back home," she said nearly an hour later as she slipped into the bathroom for a quick shower—and she didn't come back out until she was fully clothed this time. Totally satiated, yet on the verge of shedding her clothes and hopping right back into bed with him. He looked so sexy there, head propped up on one arm, chest muscles just rippling. So he was a paraplegic. No big deal, especially in the way he'd made love to her. And for a moment she wondered how many women he'd pleased the way he'd pleased her. "Well, I've really got to go now."

"You sure?"

She nodded. "I'm sure, so don't try and convince me to stay."

"Was I so good that now you're afraid of me?"

"You were," she answered directly. And that was the truth. He scared her because she was beginning to care too much. Even after all her vows not to do so, she was doing it, and she was too weak to resist him. "You make me feel things and do things I vow I won't, then you crook that little finger of yours and…" She shrugged. "Look what happens."

She buttoned her light pink blouse up to her throat

and stepped into light gray shoes to match her suit. "I need time to think, Marc. When we get back I need time to think."

"You've got all the time in the world."

"But do I?"

"I'm not going anywhere, Anne." Truth was, he needed that same time to think.

"Enjoy it while you can," she whispered to herself as the elevator opened to her. Definitely, she would enjoy it while she could.

It had been a couple of days since they'd come back from the symposium, and while they had greeted each other coming and going in the hallway, Marc had been too busy to catch a breath, let alone pay any real attention to Anne. His new physical rehab room was getting ready to open, and he was busy attending to every last detail of it. The carpenters had made quick work of the construction and now it was up to Marc to take it from there.

So the hospital was humming with activity day and night, and for most of those hours, Anne worked, too. Taking her share of their agreed-upon time to think. She simply didn't know if she wanted to get any more involved with Marc than she was already. He was such a valiant man one moment, then the anger came out in him, and he wasn't willing to try to fix that. Maybe that's what scared her most.

Part of her wanted to be involved, though. In fact, most of her wanted to, but she was also afraid of where it could take her. The road certainly wasn't clear. Not for her, anyway, but she did so want to see around the next curve. See what was or wasn't there.

Perhaps that would happen, but so far there had been no indication it would. It was work as usual. Actually, harder than usual, as Marc was totally invested in getting his physical therapy area up and operational. So who was she to complain or feel neglected? As that's the way she herself was most of the time—business first. Now she was getting a dose of her own medicine, and finding that her mind was slipping back to the weekend far more often than it should.

"You seem preoccupied," Hannah said one evening when Anne stopped by to see the baby.

"Maybe I am a little."

"Nice weekend? We haven't really talked since then."

"It was a good seminar. Ran into several old friends, learned a lot."

"I understand Marc was with you." She gave her that look that told Anne her sister already knew something was going on.

"He was."

"And?"

"He didn't attend as much of the seminar as I'd hoped he would, but he did attend some."

"And?"

"And what?"

"Did you two, well...you know? I mean, I heard about the incident in the swimming pool, so I'm only assuming that..."

"What if we did?"

Hannah grabbed her sister and hugged her. "It's about time. I was so afraid you'd give up."

"Trust me, I haven't. Marc was...incredible. But he scares me. He can be so near, then so distant, and I don't need another relationship like that. Bill was distant and

I didn't ever see it, so what does that say for me if I get involved with someone who's obviously distant?"

"So you're solving your problem with him by, what? Staying distant yourself? It doesn't work, Anne. You're at the point in your relationship now when you should be getting closer."

"I know I should, but I'm not even sure if there's a relationship."

"And you're too afraid to find out."

"What if it is?" Anne asked. "What if he expects something from me? Something I just can't give him?"

"Which would be what? Your complete trust?"

Anne nodded.

"Give him the benefit of the doubt before you toss him aside. He's not Bill and he doesn't come with a warning label that because he's a man he's destined to cheat. Real men don't cheat, Anne. That's a lesson you haven't learned yet."

"Why are you always so smart?" Anne asked.

"It's not that I'm so smart, so much as you're just wounded. Something bad happened to you once, but that's over now. You need to let go of it and look for something good. For Marc to get you so stirred up, I have to think that he's worth the effort."

Anne laughed, but sadly. "I could, but what happens once he's back in the swing of things...? He's a handsome man. Women look. Wheelchair or not, he could—"

"Don't say it, Anne. Because if you do, you doom yourself to not trusting any man ever again. Give Marc a chance to prove himself to you before you run so far away he can't catch you. Or any other man in the future if Marc doesn't turn out to be the one."

Anne gave her sister a kiss on the cheek. "The trouble with being a twin is that they know you so well."

"That's also the best part," Hannah reminded her. "So for now my sisterly advice is that you're the one he's looking at. Look back." Hannah smiled sympathetically. "And make it a good, long look. Now, how about some lemonade? Made fresh this afternoon."

"I'd love some," Anne replied. Although her mind wasn't on lemonade. It was on Marc and all the things she couldn't allow herself to have with him. Things that made her feel sad and melancholy. Things that hurt to the bone. Sure, it was easy enough for Hannah to see the problems and point them out, then give her encouragement. But seeing and acting were two different things. Hannah made perfect sense, but sense didn't always overcome fear.

"Mr. Ramsey is doing better," Marc commented to Anne after the weekly staff meeting. "He's not so depressed that it affects his therapy, which means he's making progress." Joe Ramsey had lost an arm to the war, which had been a devastating blow for an auto mechanic. "You've done a good job with him."

"Thank you," Anne said. She was genuinely pleased with his compliment. "After he's learned to use his prosthesis, I think he'll be a good candidate for vocational retraining."

"In a couple months, maybe," Marc responded.

"That long?" They were ambling along the corridor that passed Marc's new physical therapy area. Not touching or anything, but strolling close enough to each other that to an outsider they took on the appearance of intimacy.

"I want to make sure all the damage is repaired before we send him on down to start a new life completely. He's doing well with both of us. The prosthetics people teaching him how to use his new arm say he's getting more cooperative by the day, but the thing is, I don't want to push him out into the real world too prematurely. It's a scary place out there when you're forced to start over and, from what I can tell, he doesn't have much of a support system in place."

"Was it scary for you?"

"Horrifying. I'd practically pushed away all my support system and I felt so…vulnerable. I mean, I was working toward something new, but it still scared me. What if I failed? What would I have then?"

"How did you get over it?"

"The same way I get over everything—I apply myself even harder to my work. It's all I can count on."

"That's kind of sad in a way. There are lots of people out there who want to help you."

"But for how long? How long until my disability becomes a burden to them?"

"If they truly care, never." She laid a comforting hand on his shoulder. "But a lot of that's up to you, Marc, because you do the pushing first."

"I like your honesty," he said, then chuckled. "Most of the time. Anyway, about our patient…it won't hurt to keep him here a little longer than necessary so he won't have to deal with everything all at once."

Anne was impressed by his compassion and understanding of his patient. It was a side of Marc that didn't come out publicly. More than that, she was impressed by his honesty with her. It couldn't have been easy, admitting he'd been scared, maybe still was. But talking to others being treated by him, and judging from what she was learning, it was consistent. He had great empathy for wounded warriors.

She sighed and smiled, thinking about the way this awesome man kept himself hidden. "How's your physical therapy department coming along?" Anne asked Marc as they approached his door.

"I couldn't ask for a nicer setup. I've got my programs back up and running, got my rooms configured the way I want them, and things are working out well for my patients, especially now that I can separate them into like situations."

He was genuinely happy with everything. What perplexed him, though, was Anne. She'd been standoffish since they'd returned from the seminar over a week ago. She wouldn't meet his gaze when they encountered each other in the hall, had barely spoken until just now, and if he weren't mistaken, there'd been several times when he'd seen her turn and take another hall when she'd been coming toward him. What was up with that? Reluctance or embarrassment? He hoped the latter but feared the former.

Maybe this was her trying to make it up to him. Get things back to where they'd been before, which was a crazy mishmash of emotions. "Care to grab a cup of coffee?" he finally asked her before he entered his therapy room.

"I'm awfully busy today. Maybe after work?" she asked.

"After work," he agreed, hoping she meant it. *Really* hoping.

"He's a mild case, but it's affecting his progress in rehab. He'll regain his ability to walk again, maybe with some assistance for a while, but his emotions are keeping him from progressing and I thought maybe if you'd have a look at him…" Marc handed the chart over to Anne. "Then at your earliest convenience we could compare notes and see what we can come up with."

Anne took the notes and had a cursory glance at them. "I'll read them over lunch and maybe by end of day I'll have a better idea of where he might fit into the program. Will that work for you?"

"No hurry. He's pretty cooperative and very quiet, so I wouldn't put him at the top of the emergency list. Maybe over that cup of coffee later today we talked about."

"I'll call you and let you know my time frame."

Which she did three hours later.

They met at a little coffee shop a block from the rehab center and took a seat by the front window. It was early, just after four, but the shop was practically deserted.

"So, did you look at the file?" Marc asked.

She nodded. "He's withdrawn, which is something I can deal with. But he needs a regular exercise regime for the stiffness in his back and shoulders."

"Percussive injury. He took a pretty bad beating when his transport truck overturned. And while his injury isn't long-term, we can work the stiffness out of him."

"In the swimming pool?" she asked, taking a sip of her mocha latte. "I still think you could utilize it more with your patients, and Mr. Westfall is a good example of that."

"So you're into diagnosing physical therapy now?" Marc asked.

She took sudden offense that another argument was about to ensue. "I'm an internal medicine specialist, so I have made referrals from time to time. So, yes, I'm into diagnosing now. Always have been."

"I don't need your physical therapy referrals," he said, his voice a little louder than it should be.

"I thought this was a two-way street, that we both make referrals as we see fit."

"That's all you've wanted from me from day one— to make a referral for my own treatment for PTSD. Admit it!"

"Do I think you need counseling? Yes, I do, and your hair-trigger temper is a good example of that. Get anywhere close to what you perceive as therapy for you and you go off, whether or not it was really meant to be about you. Which in this case it wasn't. So I do see classic signs in you. But I haven't made a referral that involves you and I won't because you're my colleague, not someone assigned to my care."

"Even though you want to!"

"You're wrong. My patients all *want* to be cured, they don't want to hang onto all the different symptoms of PTSD and use them as an excuse for not moving forward."

"So you're implying I do."

"What I'm implying is that you know yourself and your motivations better than I do. And here's the thing, Marc. You and you alone have to want to get through it before I'd even consider making a referral, and it would have to be you coming to me and asking."

"Now, let me ask you this! Is that why we were just a one-night stand?" he said in a voice much too loud in the small shop. "You're afraid of me? Maybe you don't want to be burdened by a man in a wheelchair? Is that it, Anne? Is that why you've been avoiding me?"

"I've been avoiding you because I've already had a man with his own kind of volatile nature. He yelled at me all the time and tore up my house when I confronted him about his affairs. He tried to make me the guilty party in the failure of our marriage and for a while I accepted that because I wasn't home enough. But he knew that going in, and he almost made it my fault. Almost. And I can't do that again, because it scares me. You scare me. You thinking that I'm covertly trying to give you therapy scares me. I do care about you, Marc. Deeply. Maybe I'm even falling in love with you, but you're up and down and I just can't handle that."

"Then that's why you want to treat me as one of your patients? So you can mold me into whatever you want in a man?"

"That's not fair. I haven't tried molding you into anything. And it's just like I said, you think I'm trying to turn you into one of my patients, but I'm not. I promise you, I'm not."

"Except when it comes to swimming."

"That's encouragement, and there's a huge difference between that and what you think I'm trying to do. You have natural grace and talent, which you underutilize. Or maybe it scares you that you can still be so good at something. I don't know which it is, but there's something holding you back, and I think it's you. Besides, it was only a suggestion that you're blowing way out of proportion."

"Get me in the pool, get another of my patients in the pool. Start a world-class swim team? That's what's being blown out of proportion."

"Because you'll succeed, or because you'll fail? Are you afraid of success?" she asked. "You take your steps grudgingly because you don't think you deserve anything more?"

Marc banged his fist so hard on the table it knocked over her cup of latte, spilling it all down the front of her white blouse. "I'm sorry, Anne," he said, his voice now more subdued. "I didn't mean to—"

"You need to get some help for that temper of yours, Marc." She stood and went to the counter to get some napkins to blot her blouse. Then she came back to the table to retrieve her purse. "You lost it today with me, and I understand the cause. But what if I were someone else? A patient, maybe another doctor? You'd lose your position at the rehab center and there's a good chance you'd also lose your license to practice medicine. So you wondered why I stayed away? It's because I knew this was inevitable. Problem is, there's more where that came from."

She reached down and squeezed his hand. "Oh, and just so you'll know in advance, you're not getting my space. You may scare me in a relationship but you don't scare me as a colleague. And I'm holding onto my office."

Stepping back, Anne headed to the door, leaving Marc sitting there alone. Her heart went out to him, but until he was convinced he was worth taking the risk for, she wasn't going to pursue anything more than a professional relationship with him. That's the only thing she could do. That, and hope.

Marc was up all night, thinking. Regretting. Rethinking. Somewhere in all that mess he'd made of things yesterday she'd said she might love him. But she was afraid of him. Which he deserved, because there were times he scared himself, like yesterday at the coffee shop. The way he'd behaved…there was no excuse for that. Anne had only been trying to help him, and he'd exploded, said terrible things, made horrid accusations. And deep down he knew that all she wanted to do was help him because she cared.

Well, he cared, too. But he didn't know what to do with it or about it. Maybe he was afraid of failure. Or, worse, of success. What would happen if he did succeed with her? Would he feel backed into a corner at some point and push her away, like he had everyone else? Actually, he was almost there. If Anne didn't have the patience of a saint, she would already have been long gone. And there was the failure she talked about. The one he brought on himself.

He truly was paralyzed, and it had nothing to do with his legs.

"Someone needs to kick me hard, Sarge," he told his cat. "She's reached out to me in so many ways and I keep pushing her back. And she's so vulnerable when it comes to relationships because of her ex." Sighing heavily, he picked up his cell phone to call her but he lacked the nerve to go through with it.

"She's right, you know," he said to his very unconcerned feline. "I do need help because I do have a pretty low tolerance point. And it's time for me to start moving in the right direction. If I get the girl in the bargain, life will be perfect. If I don't, at least I won't be spending the rest of my life like Sisyphus, always pushing that boulder up the hill."

Finally finding the courage, he punched in Anne's

phone number, and when she said hello, he said two words and two words only. "You're right." Then he clicked off and waited for his new day to begin.

Anne paced up and down the hall, until Hannah finally made her take a seat in the doctors' lounge. "He's going to be fine, Anne. Give him time. This is only his first session, and Walt Anderson is a good doctor. He'll get to the bottom of what's bothering Marc."

She smiled, but impatiently. "I want it to help him, and I'm just afraid he's going to revert back to his belligerent self. But Marc's had a good hard look at himself now and he knows he's so close to the surface. I think it scares him." She stood up to pace again, but her sister pulled her back down. "The thing is, Hannah, I was so afraid I was going to lose him."

"As a patient or as the man you fell in love with?"

"Maybe both. We haven't gotten that far in our relationship yet to be able to sort it all out."

"Give it time, you will."

"I hope so because...well, you know why."

"Yes, I do know why, but do you?"

"Because I love him?" Anne said, her voice quiet and reverent. "Don't know why, don't know how, but he slipped in there."

"And it scares you?"

Anne nodded. "He's so broken."

"And you don't think the love of a good woman would go a long way in helping to fix him?"

"If he wants that love."

"He's seeking counseling because of that love. It might take a while, but he's taken the first step. Now it's time for you to do the same. Talk to him, Anne. Don't fight, don't diagnose. Just talk."

She sighed. "What if love isn't enough?"

"But what if it is?"

"You talking about me?" Marc said, pushing through the lounge door.

"And this is where I take my exit and go to my doctor's appointment," Hannah said, standing. She gave her sister a hug, then hurried out the door.

"How did it go?" Anne asked him.

"It was brutal."

Anne blanched but said nothing. Right now it was time to listen.

"But Walt says there's hope for me. He wants to see me three times a week privately."

"No group sessions?"

Marc shook his head. "Because I'm on staff here and he wants to maintain that line of separation. But he did say I could bring a guest."

"Are you going to?" she asked anxiously.

"Depends whether or not you want to come with me. As my support structure, though, not as my therapist."

"Why me?"

"Because I recognize we've got something, but we need to work through it to come out whole on the other end. I need you there, Anne, to hold me up. I'm still not sure how my real life's going to work as a disabled person, but if you want to be part of my life in spite of my disability…"

"I do," she whispered, batting back the tears threatening to spill. "I do so very much."

"Then you love me?" he asked.

Her smile for him melted. "I love you." And she sat

down on his lap and put her arms around his neck. "But the question is…"

"Yes, I love you. Have from the start but I couldn't believe that someone like me would ever have a chance with someone like you. I think I'd given up on that aspect of my life."

"Oh, because of your temper?" she whispered as she bent so that her lips brushed his. "So now's as good a time as any to tell you I've had the architects evaluate *your* office for private exam rooms, and they're working on the preliminary drawings right now."

"And where would my office go?"

"There's a large janitorial closet at the end of the hall…" She laughed. "See, I told you you wouldn't beat me at this. I get what I want."

"And what else do you want?"

"You," she whispered. "Only you."

"Then kiss me, will you?"

"Gladly. Every day for the rest of our lives."

"Go!" Anne shouted from the stands as Marc traversed the length of the pool against five other competitors. Lately he'd been swimming competitively, sometimes coming in second, occasionally third, but most often first. He'd collected a few trophies and some ribbons and the local newspaper had even done a write-up about the paralyzed swimmer who was taking para-athletics by storm. Not only that, he'd started a small swim team at the rehab center and was getting them ready for their first meet. Life was great.

"You're going to do it!" she yelled over the voices of the other spectators. "Almost there. Give it one final push and… Yay!"

She ran down to the side of the pool and took his wheelchair along so he could climb out of the water, then gave him a great big kiss on the lips. "That's three firsts in a row!" she exclaimed breathlessly.

"Want to compete with me now?" he asked, chuckling as he dried off his hair.

"Oh, I've got some competition in mind, but that will keep for later."

Later... Marc loved that word because there was a later in his life. One he'd never thought he'd have and one he would cherish every day of his life. Life didn't get better than that.

* * * * *

MILLS & BOON®
Hardback – March 2015

ROMANCE

The Taming of Xander Sterne	Carole Mortimer
In the Brazilian's Debt	Susan Stephens
At the Count's Bidding	Caitlin Crews
The Sheikh's Sinful Seduction	Dani Collins
The Real Romero	Cathy Williams
His Defiant Desert Queen	Jane Porter
Prince Nadir's Secret Heir	Michelle Conder
Princess's Secret Baby	Carol Marinelli
The Renegade Billionaire	Rebecca Winters
The Playboy of Rome	Jennifer Faye
Reunited with Her Italian Ex	Lucy Gordon
Her Knight in the Outback	Nikki Logan
Baby Twins to Bind Them	Carol Marinelli
The Firefighter to Heal Her Heart	Annie O'Neil
Thirty Days to Win His Wife	Andrea Laurence
Her Forbidden Cowboy	Charlene Sands
The Blackstone Heir	Dani Wade
After Hours with Her Ex	Maureen Child

MEDICAL

Tortured by Her Touch	Dianne Drake
It Happened in Vegas	Amy Ruttan
The Family She Needs	Sue MacKay
A Father for Poppy	Abigail Gordon

MILLS & BOON®
Large Print – March 2015

ROMANCE

A Virgin for His Prize	Lucy Monroe
The Valquez Seduction	Melanie Milburne
Protecting the Desert Princess	Carol Marinelli
One Night with Morelli	Kim Lawrence
To Defy a Sheikh	Maisey Yates
The Russian's Acquisition	Dani Collins
The True King of Dahaar	Tara Pammi
The Twelve Dates of Christmas	Susan Meier
At the Chateau for Christmas	Rebecca Winters
A Very Special Holiday Gift	Barbara Hannay
A New Year Marriage Proposal	Kate Hardy

HISTORICAL

Darian Hunter: Duke of Desire	Carole Mortimer
Rescued by the Viscount	Anne Herries
The Rake's Bargain	Lucy Ashford
Unlaced by Candlelight	Various
The Warrior's Winter Bride	Denise Lynn

MEDICAL

A Secret Shared...	Marion Lennox
Flirting with the Doc of Her Dreams	Janice Lynn
The Doctor Who Made Her Love Again	Susan Carlisle
The Maverick Who Ruled Her Heart	Susan Carlisle
After One Forbidden Night...	Amber McKenzie
Dr Perfect on Her Doorstep	Lucy Clark

MILLS & BOON®
Hardback – April 2015

ROMANCE

The Billionaire's Bridal Bargain	Lynne Graham
At the Brazilian's Command	Susan Stephens
Carrying the Greek's Heir	Sharon Kendrick
The Sheikh's Princess Bride	Annie West
His Diamond of Convenience	Maisey Yates
Olivero's Outrageous Proposal	Kate Walker
The Italian's Deal for I Do	Jennifer Hayward
Virgin's Sweet Rebellion	Kate Hewitt
The Millionaire and the Maid	Michelle Douglas
Expecting the Earl's Baby	Jessica Gilmore
Best Man for the Bridesmaid	Jennifer Faye
It Started at a Wedding...	Kate Hardy
Just One Night?	Carol Marinelli
Meant-To-Be Family	Marion Lennox
The Soldier She Could Never Forget	Tina Beckett
The Doctor's Redemption	Susan Carlisle
Wanted: Parents for a Baby!	Laura Iding
His Perfect Bride?	Louisa Heaton
Twins on the Way	Janice Maynard
The Nanny Plan	Sarah M. Anderson

MILLS & BOON®
Large Print – April 2015

ROMANCE

Taken Over by the Billionaire	Miranda Lee
Christmas in Da Conti's Bed	Sharon Kendrick
His for Revenge	Caitlin Crews
A Rule Worth Breaking	Maggie Cox
What The Greek Wants Most	Maya Blake
The Magnate's Manifesto	Jennifer Hayward
To Claim His Heir by Christmas	Victoria Parker
Snowbound Surprise for the Billionaire	Michelle Douglas
Christmas Where They Belong	Marion Lennox
Meet Me Under the Mistletoe	Cara Colter
A Diamond in Her Stocking	Kandy Shepherd

HISTORICAL

Strangers at the Altar	Marguerite Kaye
Captured Countess	Ann Lethbridge
The Marquis's Awakening	Elizabeth Beacon
Innocent's Champion	Meriel Fuller
A Captain and a Rogue	Liz Tyner

MEDICAL

It Started with No Strings...	Kate Hardy
One More Night with Her Desert Prince...	Jennifer Taylor
Flirting with Dr Off-Limits	Robin Gianna
From Fling to Forever	Avril Tremayne
Dare She Date Again?	Amy Ruttan
The Surgeon's Christmas Wish	Annie O'Neil

MILLS & BOON®

Why shop at millsandboon.co.uk?

Each year, thousands of romance readers find their perfect read at millsandboon.co.uk. That's because we're passionate about bringing you the very best romantic fiction. Here are some of the advantages of shopping at www.millsandboon.co.uk:

* **Get new books first**—you'll be able to buy your favourite books one month before they hit the shops

* **Get exclusive discounts**—you'll also be able to buy our specially created monthly collections, with up to 50% off the RRP

* **Find your favourite authors**—latest news, interviews and new releases for all your favourite authors and series on our website, plus ideas for what to try next

* **Join in**—once you've bought your favourite books, don't forget to register with us to rate, review and join in the discussions

Visit **www.millsandboon.co.uk**
for all this and more today!